A DIAGNOSIS OF MURDER

A Charley Hall Mystery, Book 3

Brenda Gayle

BowSTRING
BOOKS

BOWSTRING
BOOKS

A Diagnosis of Murder
(A Charley Hall Mystery, Book 3)
by Brenda Gayle

Published Internationally by Bowstring Books
Ottawa, Ontario, Canada
Copyright © 2020 Brenda G Heald
Print Edition Copyright © 2021 Brenda G Heald

EBOOK ISBN 978-1-9990185-8-0
PRINT ISBN 978-1-7775824-3-2

For everyone and who we were before the world changed.

"HALL!"

Charley's head snapped up as Managing Editor John Sherman's demand for her attention reverberated around the newsroom.

Now what?

It was late on a Friday afternoon in August. She had finished editing the copy for the women's section of the weekend edition of the *Kingston Tribune* newspaper and was about to send it off to the typesetter.

Editing the women's pages wasn't Charley's ideal job, but it was all she had while she waited for Lester Pyne to mess up enough for Sherman to give her back her old position as city reporter. Sometimes she was lucky and she was able to work in a story of real significance, such as last month when she'd profiled an unwed mother who'd been forced into poverty because of government bureaucracy and the strict societal norms of her class. The result had been a cascade of events that had resulted in four deaths. This week's edition was more mundane. It included a look at the wives of the men vying to be leader of the federal Liberal party, a nurses' reunion, a fundraiser tea hosted by the Imperial Order Daughters of the Empire (*thanks, Gran*), and various engagement and wedding announcements.

Charley followed Sherman into his office. Lester Pyne was lounging comfortably on the couch, shrouded in a cloud of smoke from the Chesterfield-brand cigarette he held between his tobacco-stained fingers. She remained standing while Sherman circled his desk and sat down.

"What's up, boss?" she asked.

"Pyne, here, has heard some chatter on the police scanner. There's been an incident involving some of the nurses who are in town this week. I think you should check it out."

"Why me?" Charley swung around and glared at Pyne. She knew why. It was five-thirty on a Friday and Pyne could not wait to clock out.

"You were covering those nurses, weren't you?" Pyne said.

"I included a notice of their reunion, which was provided by them, but that's all," she said. "That's hardly what I'd call 'covering' them."

"Still, it's your story," Sherman insisted.

She blew out her impatience. "What is the incident?"

"A bunch were taken to emergency at Kingston General Hospital, that's all I heard," Pyne said. "Probably an excess of excitement. You know how women can be?"

An excess of excitement?

She ignored Pyne. He wasn't worth her trouble. But Sherman? He should know better. She rounded on her boss. "I do know how women can be and I doubt very much any excess of excitement warrants a trip to the hospital emergency."

"You know what I mean," Pyne said defensively, rising from the couch and approaching Sherman's desk.

"I have no idea what you mean," Charley said keeping her focus on Sherman.

"Look, Hall, be a pal and check it out, okay? It's probably nothing, but just in case it isn't, I don't want to be scooped." There was nothing John Sherman hated more than to see the *Trib*'s rival newspaper, *The Kingston Whig-Standard*, run a story he'd missed.

"Fine," she acquiesced. Her only plan for the evening was playing a few hands of cribbage with Gran, anyway. "But if it turns into something big, I get to keep it. *Capiche?*" She waited for the managing editor to accept her demand. He had a habit of passing her leads on to Pyne. She doubted this was going to amount to a reportable story but, as Sherman said, "just in case."

———

EXCESS OF EXCITEMENT.

The expression still gnawed at her as she pushed open the doors to the emergency room of KGH—Kingston General Hospital.

Ridiculous.

At the moment, she was suffering from an excess of irritation. So much so, she didn't even notice police constables Marillo and Adams as she stalked across the lobby toward the intake desk. It wasn't until she heard Marillo call her name that she paused and turned back to them.

"The nurse isn't going to give you anything," Adams, the younger officer, said.

"How do you know?" She found Adams' superior attitude difficult to take at the best of times. "You don't even know why I'm here."

"Probably the same reason as the other hack." Adams pointed to a man Charley recognized as a reporter from the *Whig-Standard.*

Darn it!

"What can you tell me about what happened?" she asked.

Adams cocked his head to the side and allowed his gaze to roam the full five-foot-seven length of her. Charley bore his scrutiny without flinching. She had rebuffed his advances in the past. Today would be no different.

"Knock it off, kid." Constable Marillo swatted his partner's shoulder. "I think you could help us, Mrs. Hall, if you're willing."

"I'm always happy to help Kingston PD." She liked Marillo. He was a fair and decent cop who took the job, but not himself, seriously. It was too bad he had to be paired up with a pompous ass like Adams.

"The other nurses, the ones not admitted, are in a room through there." Marillo pointed at a swinging door where another uniformed police officer was stationed. "It would be helpful if you could speak with them, see if you can find out what happened."

"Won't they talk to you?"

"We tried, but they are terribly upset. The uniform seems to intimidate them. They're not in trouble or anything, but I can't make much sense out of what they've told me."

"Okay, I'll talk to them, but first, tell me what you do know. These are the nurses who were here for a reunion, correct? There are twelve of them."

"Yeah." He glanced down at his notepad and frowned. "I've counted nine. One arrived unconscious and three others were complaining of nausea and stomach pain. Five more are in that room, along with a chaperone. All we've got out of them, so far, is that they've been together—all of them —for the past two-and-a-half days."

"If that's the case, why would only four be afflicted?"

"And that is what we want you to help us figure out," Marillo said.

"It's possible the four weren't with the others *all* the time, and the other girls are covering for them," Adams interjected with a not-so-subtle suggestion of a more nefarious reason for their distress.

"I think they might feel more comfortable opening up to a woman," Marillo added, apparently supporting his partner's theory.

"And in return?" She would do it regardless, but it would be so much better if she could get a scoop out of it, too.

"In return, you get the satisfaction of knowing you are doing your civic duty by helping local law enforcement," Marillo said. "To be crystal clear, Mrs. Hall, nothing is on the record until we determine what happened to those girls."

Six pairs of eyes turned toward Charley as she stepped into the room and then widened in panic at the sight of the two uniformed officers who followed her. Charley turned back to the cops. "Do you need to stay?"

"One of us does," Marillo replied. He gestured to Adams. "Wait outside."

"Can you spot me a coin for a cup of coffee?" Adams asked. "Or maybe a buck so I can get something to go with it. I'm missing my dinner."

Marillo scowled but dug into his pocket and handed him a banknote. "Here, take a fiver. Get something for me, too, will ya?"

Inside the room, Charley introduced herself as a friend of the police and asked if she might sit with the nurses. "Constable Marillo's a good guy, but you don't have to talk to him. He's here to listen. You can talk to me," she said, placing herself between two of the young women sitting on the sofa.

"Are you going to publish what we say?" asked a woman with silver threads running through her dark hair. She looked quite a bit older than the others and recognized Charley's name.

"I'm not here as a reporter. Constable Marillo thought

you might prefer to talk to another woman about what happened."

"You're not going to report on it, then?" the woman asked again.

Charley hesitated. That was why she had come, after all. "I want to help the police figure out what happened to your colleagues. But you're right, if it's newsworthy, I would like to write about it. That is my job. But it's entirely up to you whether that happens." She glanced around the room. "I won't reveal anything you say here unless you give me permission. Okay?" She turned back to the older woman. "Right now, all we want is to help your friends."

"I don't know what we can tell you." The dark-haired woman seemed to have appointed herself spokesperson for the group.

"Why don't we start with your names?" Normally Charley would have taken out her notebook by now and be scribbling information, but in this instance, she was certain that would be a mistake. She glanced back at Marillo and saw that he was of a similar mind.

Well, then. Charley prided herself on having a good memory, and now it would be put to the test. Between her and Marillo, surely they'd be able to recollect whatever information the nurses gave them.

Charley was correct: the older, dark-haired woman, Mrs. Bowman, wasn't a graduate nurse. She was the head of the local alumnae association that had arranged the reunion of the previous year's graduates. The others—Margaret, Catherine, Nancy, Donna and Laura—were five of the twelve nurses who had attended. With four admitted to hospital, that left three unaccounted for.

"Alice and Ramona have husbands at home and, given all the commotion, asked to leave the reunion to return to them," Mrs. Bowman said. "And Betty, poor dear, is six months pregnant and has taken to her bed due to the shock of it all."

"Are you all from Kingston and the area?" Charley asked.

"Oh, no. Margaret and Catherine live in Ottawa, Nancy is in Toronto, and Donna moved to Syracuse last month, didn't you dear?"

The young woman nodded. "But my mam is here, so I expect I'll be coming home to visit quite often."

"How nice for you. And isn't that wonderful that the whole graduating class could come back," Charley said with a smile.

Several of the nurses lowered their eyes and others darted anxious looks at Mrs. Bowman.

"Well, there are two who didn't make it," Mrs. Bowman said. "But twelve out of fourteen is an excellent turnout."

A blush crept up the cheek of the young woman to Charley's right—Nancy—and she wasn't the only one. As Charley glanced around the room, none of the nurses would meet her eye. Something more was going on.

"Mrs. Bowman," Marillo said from the corner, "there is still quite a bit of paperwork the hospital needs concerning the young women you brought in. I promised the intake nurse that I would ask for your assistance at the earliest convenience. I wonder if you'd accompany me now?"

"Now?"

"Yes, now." Marillo's tone was firm. He held open the door, giving the woman no option but to comply.

Charley silently thanked Marillo for his perceptiveness. There was no way the young women were going to open up to her with Mrs. Bowman in the room. Once the door closed, they took a collective sigh and their shoulders relaxed.

"Off the record, what is the real reason the other women didn't come to the reunion?" Charley kept her voice light, surely some of these nurses were fond of engaging in a little gossip.

"Well, Sharon is due to have a baby any day now, so of course she couldn't come," the woman sitting to Charley's left—Laura?—said.

Charley waited to reply. It was a trick she often employed. Most people couldn't stand silence and rushed to fill it—often revealing more than they'd intended. In less than a minute, three voices filled the void, speaking in rapid succession.

"Adeline is Adeline and she'll do as she pleases."

"Yes, her absence is no great loss."

"Frankly, I was relieved when I arrived and learned she wouldn't be joining us."

"Does this Adeline live in Kingston?" Charley asked.

"Oh, yes," Laura said. "But she married right after we graduated and has never worked as a nurse, which I am sure is to the benefit of all patients."

"No empathy in that one," the freckled-faced redhead from Syracuse—Donna?—said. "Remember the time she told the poor old dear, who was about to lose his leg, to buck up and be happy he was going to live?"

"And that he could have avoided the whole thing if he'd bothered to see the doctor *before* the gangrene set in." Nancy shook her head in disgust. "Imagine!"

"Apparently she's off to Ottawa for the convention this weekend," Margaret said from across the room. "Frankly, I couldn't wait to get out of there—all those highfalutin so-and-sos preening like peacocks, all to impress one another."

"She'll fit right in then, won't she?" Laura giggled.

Charley nodded in agreement. She knew precisely what convention Margaret was referring to. The federal Liberal party was poised to elect its first new leader in twenty-nine years. It was a big deal. The winner would immediately become the country's prime minister, replacing William Lyon Mackenzie King. Her close childhood friend, Alderman Dan Cannon, was one of the highfalutin so-and-sos who had gone to Ottawa as a delegate. Charley was a little surprised he hadn't asked her to accompany him as he usually did; but then again, she'd never said yes in the past, so maybe he'd finally given up on her.

"Do you remember when she got her ring that Christmas?" Donna asked. "And how she used to parade around as if she was so much better than us?"

"La-di-da, I'm going to be Mrs. Colin Banks," Nancy sang as she fluttered her fingers to show off an imaginary ring.

Charley grinned along with them. She had gained their trust. Now, she could ask about what had happened to their classmates.

"Aside from this Adeline, it seems you all get along pretty well," she said.

"Mostly." Laura shrugged.

"As well as a dozen young ladies forced to live and work together ever do," Donna agreed.

"Can you tell me what happened to your friends?" Charley asked.

"We don't know. We were finishing our tea when Wendy said she wasn't feeling well and went to lie down in the sitting room," Laura said. "A short time later, Peg and Debbie started complaining about the heat and how they were having trouble breathing."

"What made you come to the hospital?"

"I couldn't wake Wendy when it was time to leave. When I went in, her face was pale and her skin waxy. Her breathing was shallow and when I checked her pulse..." Laura shook her head. "Bradycardia."

"Her heartbeat was very slow," Donna explained.

"By this time, Susan—she was at a different table from the others—was feeling especially poorly, too," Nancy interrupted, "and so Mrs. Bowman thought we should bring the whole lot in to be checked."

"Do you think it could be something you ate?" Charley asked.

The women glanced at each other and shook their heads. "We all ate the same thing," Laura said.

"Tell me about the tea," Charley asked. "Who arranged it? What was served?"

"It was Super's tea—" Donna began.

"Super?" Charley interrupted.

"Superintendent Marlow. She's in charge of the nursing staff here at KGH. This is where we did our training..." Donna's voice had trailed off.

"Superintendent Marlow arranged the tea and...?" Charley prompted with a nod, encouraging Donna to continue.

"Super hosted the tea and we were served by this year's class—"

"It was a regular tea with fancy sandwiches and pastries," Laura chimed in.

"Who made the food and prepared the tea?"

"The student nurses. It's tradition. We did it last year for the previous graduating class and next year's gang will do it for this year's," Laura added.

"Where was it held? You said Susan was at a different

table from the others who got sick? How many tables were there?" Charley asked.

"It was in Mrs. Pecker's dining room," Laura said.

"Mrs. Pecker was our den mother," Donna explained. "We lived at her rooming house while we were training."

"We were at three tables," Laura continued. "Wendy sat with Peg and Debbie, at Super's. I was at that table, too. But Susan was at the table hosted by Mrs. Bowman. You were with them, right Donna? Along with Betty and Ramona? Mrs. Pecker hosted the third, with Nancy, Catherine, Margaret and Alice. But no one at her table got sick."

It didn't make any sense to Charley. Why these four women? "What about earlier in the day or yesterday? Have you been together the whole time?"

"Yes, since Wednesday."

"Every meal? Every activity?"

She looked around the room as the five women nodded in agreement.

So, probably not food poisoning.

Probably not poisoning, at all.

What then? Flu?

That seemed the most plausible explanation.

Charley rose and thanked the women for their help. As she approached the door to leave, it opened and a doctor stepped into the room, followed by Constable Marillo and an ashen-faced Mrs. Bowman.

"I am sorry to have to tell you this," the doctor said, "but Miss Wendy Walker passed away a short time ago."

"CHARLEY, WAKE UP."

Charley squinted against the bright overhead lights and tried to stretch out the crick in her shoulders. The Naugahyde sofa in the emergency's waiting room, barely comfortable at the best of times, was not conducive to being used as a bed. She gratefully accepted the steaming mug of coffee Laine Black handed her.

"Have you been here all night?" Laine asked. She was dressed in the usual crisp, white coat of a hospital resident. Laine was one of a handful of women doctors in training there.

"'Fraid so." She took a sip from the mug and made a face. *Blah!* Hospital coffee was the worst.

"Not so good, is it?" Laine smirked and sat down beside her.

"I should be used to it by now, with all the time I spend here." Charley had practically lived at the hospital a few months back when her brother, Freddie, had been attacked while sailing on the lake. "Is there any news?"

"No, there's nothing for you to report on. The police left hours ago."

Charley took another sip for the caffeine hit that she

needed to function. Laine looked tired, too. "Long shift?" she asked her friend. Charley had met Laine several months earlier through Grace Fletcher, the *Tribune*'s archivist.

"A frustrating shift," the petite doctor replied. "Two of the nurses will be released this morning; they're fine, no lingering symptoms. The third, Susan..." She shrugged helplessly. "She presented with tachycardia—that's an extremely fast heartbeat—but she quickly dropped into bradycardia and started having convulsions. This was the same state Wendy Walker was in when she arrived. It was too late for her, but with this patient, we administered epinephrine to try to raise her blood pressure and she's now in a mechanical respirator."

"Do you mean an iron lung? Like they use for polio?" Charley had a friend in high school whose breathing muscles had been paralyzed by the disease. He had spent months inside the iron lung's airtight chamber, but it wasn't enough to save him.

"Yes, but it's not only used for polio. She needs help breathing right now. We're hoping it will give us more time to figure out what's going on."

"Will she recover?"

"We're doing everything we can." She sounded irritated.

"Of course," Charley said quickly. "You've ruled out poison?"

"We haven't ruled out—or in—anything. However, poison seems unlikely given what we do know. There will be an autopsy on Wendy Walker later this morning. I'll let you know if anything comes of it." She stood up. "Go home, Charley. Get a decent cup of coffee and enjoy your weekend."

"Hello?" Charley pushed open the door to the red-brick, colonial home that her grandparents had built and she'd grown up in.

"Good morning, Mrs. Hall." Rachel, her grandmother's newest housekeeper greeted her as she carried a coffee urn from the kitchen to the dining room. "I'll be right with you."

Charley liked Rachel. She was close to her own age, late twenties, and had grown up in Kingston. But that was all Charley knew about the woman and she didn't dare ask for more details. Her grandmother's inability to keep a house-keeper for any length of time was a long-standing joke Charley shared with Freddie. But the loss of the last one had been Charley's fault. Apparently, she had become too nosy and had broken some unwritten domestic staff code of conduct simply by wanting to know more about the woman who worked for her family.

In the few conversations she'd had with Rachel, Charley had gotten the sense that the woman was well-educated and had come from a good family. All Charley's reporter instincts were primed to find out why the young woman had to go into domestic service, but she didn't dare listen to them. Gran would be furious if Charley's curiosity cost them another housekeeper. Besides, she'd bet Freddie that Rachel would still be with them by Christmas—five months from now—and she needed to redeem herself after losing to him last time.

"I've just put out a fresh pot of coffee," Rachel said, taking Charley's hat and satchel. "But if you would prefer, I can deliver one up to your room. You must be tired after working all night."

Considerate and observant, too.

"Thank you, Rachel. I am exhausted, but I'll say good morning to my grandmother before taking a nap."

"There she is!" Freddie leapt from his chair and kissed Charley's cheek as she entered the dining room. "For once it's not me who's been out carousing all night."

Charley playfully swatted her brother. "Hardly carousing. I was working." She bent and kissed her grandmother's cheek. "Good morning, Gran."

"Good morning, Charlotte. I am so glad you could join us." Elizabeth Stormont—Bessie as she was known to family and friends—didn't try to disguise her sarcasm.

"Ooo hoo, look who's in trouble now." Freddie hadn't returned to his seat. He reached across the table and plucked a slice of buttered toast from the plate.

"I did call and explain where I was," Charley said, wondering why Gran was chastising her for doing her job rather than her brother for his poor table manners.

"It's not proper for a woman to be out all night," Bessie said. "I'll have to have a chat with John Sherman about it."

"You will not!" Charley glared at her grandmother. "I wasn't out wandering the streets. I was at the hospital waiting for news on some nurses who fell ill. One even died."

Gran raised her eyebrows and cocked her head at Charley's explanation. She knew it wasn't all that long ago that Charley had spent several evenings out wandering the streets and had almost gotten herself into trouble. And Charley couldn't rule out the possibility that she would do it again if she had to.

"It's my job. Please don't talk to Sherman." She cringed at how pitiful she sounded. She sometimes wondered if Bessie had used her position as the widow of the *Kingston Tribune*'s former publisher to get Charley demoted to the women's pages. Gran had often stated she would prefer it if Charley didn't work at all—an opinion she couldn't comprehend particularly given Bessie's prominent role in the fight to secure the vote for women.

"The *Lady Stonebridge* awaits and I'm off," Freddie said breaking the tension. He bent and kissed Bessie's cheek. "I'll be home for dinner."

"I think sailing has been good for him," Bessie said after he'd left.

"Hmmm." Charley took a sip of coffee. So much better than what Laine had presented her with. She had been worried when Freddie had said he was going to rehabilitate the *Lady Stonebridge*, the sloop that had belonged to her parents—the one they'd been sailing when they'd drowned twenty-five years ago. He'd told her he hoped sailing would redeem both the boat and himself—drinking, in his case— and from what she'd seen, it had been successful. He was far from the confident young man who'd left to fight the Nazis in '39, but over the past month, her brother seemed to be more at peace and in control of his drinking than he'd been since his return two years ago.

"I'm worried about the anniversary coming up."

Charley nodded. August 19th, the sixth anniversary of the Dieppe Raid, one of the darkest days of the war. Freddie had been among the almost five thousand Canadians who came ashore at different points along the coastline of occupied France. Less than half returned to England. Almost one thousand lost their lives on the beaches and another two thousand, including Freddie, were taken prisoner.

The anniversary had been in the news recently. Seventy-five soldiers and their families were returning to Dieppe to mark the occasion, which was set to include services at the Canadian cemetery and in Canada Square, the opening of a new boulevard on the esplanade near the site of the landings, and a Franco-Canadian photographic exhibition. Like Gran, Charley feared the Dieppe anniversary posed a serious threat to Freddie's new-found sobriety.

"I've already spoken with Grace and Laine, and they've both arranged to take time off work," Charley said. The two roommates were skilled sailors without a boat and Freddie had a boat but no experience. It was a match made in heaven. "The plan is to keep him sailing right through the weekend. Fingers crossed for good weather."

"That makes me feel somewhat better," Bessie said. "But what about you?"

The fatigue she'd been fighting blanketed Charley and she crumpled in her seat, no longer able to ignore her own apprehension about the day and...

Theo.

Freddie's best friend.

Her husband.

After Dieppe, they had been informed that both Freddie and Theo were missing in action and presumed dead. Her brother had mysteriously reappeared almost a year after the end of the war, revealing that he'd been in a POW camp and offering no explanation for the interval between the time the camps were liberated and his return home. But of Theo, there had been no news. Freddie couldn't—or wouldn't—tell them anything about what had happened to him. Concerned for his precarious mental state, Charley hadn't felt she could press her brother on the subject, so her life remained in limbo.

Wife or widow?

How could she move on?

She mustered up a brave front. "I'll be fine, Gran. Please don't worry about me."

In her heart of hearts, she wanted Freddie to grow stronger and recover—for himself, certainly, but also for her. If he could beat the demons that plagued him, maybe he would be able to tell her what happened to Theo.

And then, finally, she would be able to give Dan the answer he wanted.

I SHOULD HAVE ORDERED A CAR.

Charley's pace had slowed significantly. Her brisk thirty-minute walk from the *Kingston Tribune*'s offices on Bath Street to her home on King Street West had extended to more than forty minutes, and she wasn't there yet.

After a cool start to the month, a heat wave had moved in over the weekend, bringing temperatures in the mid-eighties, which was unusual for the lakeside town.

Yup, a car would have been a good idea.

She'd originally rejected the idea because she hadn't relished sitting in a hot, sticky automobile. However, in re-evaluating her decision, taking a taxi would have meant a mere ten minutes of torture rather than the forty-five she was enduring now.

She paused to switch her satchel to her other hand and removed her hat to fan her face.

And you could have stuck your head out of the window to take advantage of the air rushing by.

Charley giggled as she considered Bessie's reaction to seeing her granddaughter pulling into the laneway with her head hanging out of a car window like a panting dog. The vision gave her the burst of energy she needed to push on.

Walking was her favourite mode of transportation, and

she usually didn't mind the weather. Wind, rain, snow, it didn't bother her. Freddie had offered to teach her to drive the family car and Grace had encouraged her to get a bicycle, but neither appealed to her. She enjoyed the fresh air and the opportunity to be alone with her thoughts.

Driving or cycling would require her to pay too much attention to what was happening around her. If she became distracted while walking and occasionally veered off the sidewalk into one of the century-old hardwoods that lined the streets, the only injury would be to her ego. Just the other day, she had been mentally working through the layout of the Saturday women's pages when she'd found herself face-to-face with a yew bush. The sharp tips of its flat needles had left tiny scratches on her cheek, but that was preferable to the injuries—and deaths—she had seen when she'd had to cover automobile accidents on the city beat.

She was in the final stretch. She rounded the corner onto King Street West and—

What is he doing here?

Charley glared at the familiar black sedan parked in the laneway.

She hadn't seen Mark Spadina in more than six weeks—not since the two of them had cleared Dan of the murder charge he'd been facing. It wasn't that she was purposefully avoiding the police-officer-turned-private-detective, or he her, as far as she knew. But really, what had they in common except a penchant for solving murders? If he was at her home...

She picked up her pace.

She handed her hat and satchel to Rachel, giving the housekeeper a cursory "fine" in response to her inquiry about Charley's day.

Freddie and Mark both rose as she rushed into the drawing room. She glanced at the couch where Laine and, to her great surprise, Grace sat sipping iced tea.

"How?" she asked. Grace had still been working when she had left the *Trib*.

"Bicycle." Grace shrugged. "It was quite pleasant. Plus, it's mostly downhill, which is a tremendous advantage in this heat. You look flushed, Charley. Have some tea. It's delicious."

Charley turned her attention to Mark. "What are you doing here?"

His dark eyes creased at the corners and a crooked smile seemed to balance out his crooked nose. "And a very good afternoon, to you, too, Mrs. Hall." His deep voice held that mocking tone she found so irritating as it was usually directed at her.

She accepted the glass of iced tea Freddie had poured for her and sat down in her favourite *bergère* armchair.

"Now that we're all here—" Freddie began.

"Why are we all here?" Charley interrupted. "And where's Gran?" She glanced around the room. A private detective? A doctor? A top-notch researcher? Had something happened to Bessie?

"Gran's still at book club," Freddie said. "Look, can we—"

"What book is she reading this month?" Mark interrupted. He grinned at Charley, no doubt remembering a previous, somewhat scandalous book Bessie's club had tackled.

"*In a Lonely Place*, by Dorothy B. Hughes," Charley said. The dark crime novel was an odd choice given her grandmother's vehement opposition to Charley's involvement in murder investigations. From his raised eyebrows, Mark was surprised, too.

"Can we get back to the business at hand?" Freddie asked impatiently.

"Yes, sorry Cap'n," Mark said, leaning back and crossing his arms. "Proceed."

"I guess I should be the one to explain," Laine said. "I had told Freddie and Grace about some concerns I've been having, and they suggested, perhaps, the two of you could help."

"What sort of concerns?" Charley asked.

Laine stood and began to walk the circumference of the room. "Look, I don't know. It may be nothing. Coincidence?"

"It's not!" Freddie said. "Tell them what you told us."

She nodded and returned to her seat. "Okay." She looked at Charley. "Do you remember a few weeks ago when we had those four nurses come into emergency?"

"Yeah, one died," Charley said. She had followed up with the police the following Monday, but Constable Marillo had told her they weren't pursuing it. And Laine had said the autopsy was inconclusive. They had no idea what had caused the woman's heart to stop, so it was written off as an unexplained, but natural, death. "Two were released the next morning, and the third recovered, right?" She'd written a small two-inch notice when Susan Bowman —who it turned out was the daughter of Mrs. Bowman, the head of the nurses' alumnae association—had been released from the hospital the following week.

"Not completely recovered," Laine said. "But she's home with her family now."

"I thought that was the end of it."

"I did, too, until last week." Laine had started pacing

again. "Exactly one week later, on a Friday, two more nurses were admitted under similar circumstances—this time at Hotel Dieu hospital. Their symptoms were mild: nausea, vomiting, rapid heart rate, sweating, some breathing problems, but nothing too serious. They were released after the weekend."

"Where were they before the symptoms appeared?" Charley craned her neck to follow Laine as she walked behind the armchair.

"They were all at a baby shower for one of the nurses." Laine stopped in front of Charley. "There were ten of them. They claim they'd been there all afternoon, eating and drinking all the same things—all in the same classroom at the hospital."

"And before that?" Charley asked.

"There's nothing to link them together other than they all worked at the hospital, but not necessarily on the same shifts or in the same wards."

"And only two of the ten at the shower got sick? Didn't anyone think that was odd?"

"The doctors there couldn't find any reason for it. They've put it down to female hysteria."

"They think it's in their heads?" Charley gaped at the doctor. "Don't they see the similarities to what happened before? That first nurse who died—are they suggesting she *thought* herself to death?"

"There's a lot about the human mind that we don't know," Laine said. "But for the record, I think they're wrong. I think there is a physical cause for what happened to all those women. I just don't know what it is."

"But that's not all," Freddie prompted. "Tell them about last week."

"On Friday, for the third week in a row, we had another

woman present at KGH with these same symptoms. I wasn't working that day."

Charley remembered that both Laine and Grace had taken last Thursday and Friday off in order to be with Freddie during the Dieppe anniversary and throughout the weekend. She glanced toward her brother and uttered a small prayer of thanks to her friends. He had managed to make it through without losing himself in a bottle.

Charley hadn't fared quite as well. It had been a long, difficult four days. Between the news coverage and her own memories of the time, she'd been unable to escape the melancholy the anniversary had evoked. And Dan, the one person she had counted on to help her through it, was nowhere to be found. She hadn't seen him since he'd left for the Liberal convention earlier in the month and had only managed to speak with him on the telephone once. He'd been distracted—distant—and told her he would be in touch later.

"It wasn't until I returned to work this morning that I learned about it," Laine was continuing.

"Is she going to be okay?" Charley asked.

"No." Laine slumped down beside Grace and placed her face in her hands. Grace wrapped her arms around her and drew her close.

"She died," Grace said quietly over Laine's head.

"I'm sorry," Charley said.

Laine pushed back and sat up. She cupped Grace's cheek and nodded her appreciation for the support. "It wasn't a nurse this time." She took a deep breath. "It was a medical intern. Barbara Young. The female students in all years, including the interns and residents, get together every Friday afternoon to talk about how the week went and to offer moral support."

"So, she was also in a group when she fell ill," Charley mused, elucidating the pattern.

"There are only five of us."

Us.

The realization hit Charley like a punch to the gut. If not for Freddie, Laine would have been there, too.

"I SYMPATHIZE WITH YOU, Doc, but I'm not sure how we can help." Mark spoke for the first time. "This sounds like a medical issue."

"No," Charley said, clearly understanding why Laine was concerned. "Look at the pattern: it is always women, they are always in a group, it is always on a Friday. Things like that don't happen randomly. It has to be deliberate."

"About the only thing that is random is the number of women affected," Grace said.

"And the severity of their symptoms," Laine added.

"But how does it happen?" Charley began her own pacing of the room.

"That's what we're hoping you and Detective Spadina can figure out," Freddie said.

"The police don't think it's suspicious?" Charley asked.

Laine shook her head.

"Nah, unless a doctor specifically told them there was a crime, they'd have no reason to investigate," Mark said. "And from what you're saying, the docs at the hospital aren't prepared to call it one."

"The *male* doctors," Laine clarified for him. "The female doctors—and the nurses—are pretty scared."

"I don't know," Mark said rubbing his chin and looking

dubious. "How do you know it's not some sort of bug that is infecting women working in hospitals?"

The sound of a door opening and closing, followed by female voices in the hallway, stopped Laine from commenting. Bessie had returned.

Charley glanced toward Mark, slightly panicked. As soon as Gran saw him, she'd know something was up. Mark winked back at her as if to tell her he had the situation handled.

"Well, hello." Gran paused on the threshold of the drawing room, her gaze circling the group. Despite the heat, she wore her customary ankle-length dress with a high lace collar and long sleeves. Only the few frizzy strands of grey hair that had escaped her brioche-shaped bun seemed to give any concession to the humidity. "If I'd known we were having company, I wouldn't have dawdled at book club."

Freddie and Mark both rose with her entrance. Freddie crossed the room and kissed her cheek. "We were planning our weekend," he said. "I know it's the beginning of the week, but with everyone's busy schedules..." He shrugged.

Bessie sat down in Charley's favourite chair—the only one not occupied—and accepted the glass of iced tea Mark had poured for her. "I haven't seen you in quite some time, Detective," she said.

"It's nice to be missed." Mark had an ease with Bessie that Charley envied. Most people were intimidated by the status and stature of Elizabeth Stormont, but not him. He was always respectful, although not necessarily reverential.

"I was quite enjoying the respite." Gran loved a good sparring partner. "It meant no one had been murdered and my granddaughter wasn't about to be drawn into some sinister investigation of yours."

"I think you've been reading too many of those mystery books, Gran," Charley said.

"Well, in this case, you are incorrect, madam." Mark flashed her a broad smile, displaying his perfect teeth. "I am here to take Mrs. Hall to dinner."

"You are?" Charley gaped at him and then tried to hide her surprise, but not before she caught Mark's disapproving frown. She went to stand beside him. "I mean, of course you are. I had forgotten it was tonight, that's all." She turned to Gran. "I just got home myself."

Bessie took a long sip of her iced tea and eyed the pair suspiciously.

"We should be on our way." Mark took Charley's arm and propelled her toward the door. "Bessie, always a pleasure. Have a good evening, everyone."

———

"WHERE ARE WE GOING?" Charley asked as Mark backed his sedan out of the laneway.

"Dinner," he said. "I'm not about to lie to your grandmother. And frankly, Tiger, you need to be nimbler when you're stretching the truth with her."

"Yeah, I don't think she believed us." Oh well, it wouldn't be the first time Charley went against Gran's wishes. She was a grown woman, so why did her grandmother's opinion still matter so much to her?

"You," Mark said. "She didn't believe *you*. I could have sold it if you hadn't come across like a deer caught in the headlights."

Charley wasn't convinced. Her grandmother had demonstrated time and again the uncanny ability to unearth

Charley's secrets. "Do you want to talk about how we're going to approach Laine's case?"

"First, I want to talk about Rose Cannon and what you can do to get her off my back. She keeps asking me to come to her house for tea."

Charley sympathized with him. Dan's mother, Rose, had been sending invitations to her, too.

A few months ago, Rose had noticed the similarities between Mark and Dan. They weren't physically alike and so it wasn't immediately obvious to the casual observer. But if you saw how the two men interacted with one another—mostly how pig-headed they were—one could start to wonder. And Rose, uniquely aware that she was not Dan's biological mother, had.

Charley had rebuffed her questions. It wasn't her place to explain. Mark had asked her not to tell Dan that they were half-brothers, and she had kept his secret. But she also empathized with Rose. Her son had a half-brother, so why wouldn't she want to get to know him? Charley understood that, but Mark, raised in an orphanage, did not.

"I'm afraid you're on your own," Charley said. "When Rose gets a bee in her bonnet, it's tough to shake out."

"Hmph," Mark snorted, unconvinced but dropped the subject. He cranked the steering wheel and jerked to a stop, the tires of his automobile scraping the curb.

"We're eating here?" Charley asked, suspiciously eyeing the dirty window of the diner he'd parked in front of. With all the grime, she could barely make out the name stenciled onto the window: Joe's.

"Sorry, Tiger, but what did you expect? I am a lowly private detective. I can't afford any of those *chichi* places you're used to."

"I can pay," she offered.

"No way, no how am I taking money from a dame!"

"Oh, for heaven's sake!" Charley reluctantly got out of the car but hesitated to go inside. "It's not like it's a date or anything. You had no trouble taking my money—or Gran's —when we were working on Dan's case."

"That's different. That was a job. This is dinner. Besides, I eat here all the time." He opened the door and motioned for her to precede him inside. "The food's decent."

The inside of Joe's wasn't as bad as she feared. Across from the door, a half-dozen red-capped swivelling stools sat in front of a counter that ran the length of the room. Behind it, a small, wiry man—Joe?—wearing a sleeveless undershirt and apron, wielded a spatula over a sizzling grill. Mark touched her elbow and led her to one of the four square tables off to the side.

"You can unpucker your kisser, Tiger. It's not that bad," he whispered, pulling out her chair for her.

She picked up the fork and examined it. It looked clean. And the smell... Either she was so hungry her senses were playing tricks on her, or that wonderful aroma wafting from the grill promised a delicious meal despite the ambiance—or lack of it. She returned the fork to the table. "What do you recommend?"

"Now you're talking," he said, waving at the lone wait-ress whose tired, sweat-dampened face lit up when she saw him.

"Detective Spadina!" The woman looked to be in her mid-fifties. She wore a blue gingham dress with a discoloured and stained apron. "Who do we have here?"

"Gillian, my love, this is Mrs. Hall. A client."

Charley cast him an annoyed look. Would it be so diffi-cult to admit they were friends?

Except they weren't friends, were they? So why should she worry about how he described her to a stranger?

She pocketed her disquiet. It was another one of the many aspects about her relationship with Detective Mark Spadina she didn't understand and didn't care to explore.

"We'll have two liver and onions with whatever the daily veg is," Mark said. "And make sure you save us two big ol' slices of cherry pie with vanilla ice cream for dessert."

Charley watched Gillian walk away. What was her story? How long had she worked here? Was she married to Joe? Was there a Joe?

Mark would probably know, but there was no way she was going to ask him. He had accused her of being elitist and that is what had led to the last housekeeper quitting. If he hadn't badgered her about it, she'd never have peppered Irena with questions about her life in Poland.

His comments had stung; still did. But worse than that, they had made her question who she was as a person and where she fit in society—in the world. Now, every time she met someone, she felt compelled to ask them about themselves. Where were they from? What did they do? How did they view what was happening around them? Such curiosity was an advantage to a reporter, but she had learned the hard way that not everyone was receptive to such probing.

Mark had opened her eyes to what she considered to be a personal failing. Regardless of how uncomfortable it made her, she was grateful. But never in a million years would she admit that to him.

She turned to meet his arrogant stare. "Now, how are we going to find our murderer?"

"PLEASE LET THEM IN, Mother. I am *soooo* bored!"

Charley recognized the woman from the hospital as she stood blocking the entrance to her home. Mrs. Bowman turned back from the voice calling from inside and glared at Mark and Charley before stepping aside to let them pass.

"She's not well," Mrs. Bowman said pointing to a room on the left. "I'd appreciate it if you didn't upset her."

"That is the last thing we want to do ma'am," Mark said.

"It's nice to see you again," Charley said. Once she'd realized who Mrs. Bowman was, Charley had been impressed by how well the woman had retained her composure at the hospital even though it was her own daughter who was in critical condition. She had exuded calm control, no doubt so as not to further upset the girls in her care. Today, however, she looked tired and haggard. There were dark circles under her eyes and a furrow between her brows. The streaks of silver that had highlighted her dark hair seemed to have multiplied, making her appear much older than Charley originally imagined her to be. But who could blame her? Her daughter had been at death's door.

A young woman with dark hair and an unnaturally grey complexion broke into a huge grin as they entered the sitting room. "I saw you coming up the walk and was hoping you were here to see me," Susan Bowman said, her blue eyes dancing with delight. "Mother has scared away almost everyone I know. She's concerned, I do understand, but I am going crazy cooped up here, with just the two of us."

Charley and Mark each took an armchair across from the sofa where Susan lay wrapped in a brightly coloured quilt.

Charley hadn't known what to expect when they arrived. When she and Mark had mapped out their plan the previous evening, they'd decided to go back and examine the first incident. Susan Bowman and her mother would be their first stop.

Although Laine had warned them that Susan wasn't completely recovered, Charley was still taken aback by how frail the young woman appeared. In stark contrast, her bubbly personality seemed to belie her physical state. With any luck, that was what would get her through.

"Thank you for seeing us," Charley said after making introductions. "I spoke with your mother and the other nurses from the reunion while you were in the hospital, but I was hoping you'd be willing to answer a few questions for us."

"I don't know what more I can tell you. I was in a pretty bad way and don't remember much."

"Anything would be helpful," Mark said.

Her face clouded. "Well, it was during the Super's tea, I started feeling poorly, but you know, I tried to buck up. And then poor Wendy had to go lie down."

"She did that after you felt ill?" Charley asked.

"She was at a different table, so I don't know when she began to feel sick. I stayed where I was because I didn't want to upset Mother. I was at her table and she'd put in ever so much work arranging our reunion, you see?"

Charley turned to Mrs. Bowman. "It must have been quite an undertaking."

"It's my privilege. I do it every year."

"What can you tell us about Wendy?" Mark asked Susan. "What was she like? Was she popular with you girls?"

"Wendy was a...how to say this? She was a firecracker." Susan leaned back and chuckled to herself. "We all loved her—the other girls and me. But she wasn't one to blindly follow the rules." She glanced toward her mother, who had quietly taken a chair near the entrance to the room. "She wasn't fond of curfew, and more than once was caught sneaking back into her room after hours."

"And more than once I received a call from Mrs. Pecker advising me that she wasn't the only one," Mrs. Bowman said. "I don't want to speak ill of the dead, but Wendy Walker was a handful."

"It was all innocent fun," Susan said, giving her mother a defiant stare. "We all admired Wendy. She stood up for us with the doctors and the medical students. She wouldn't take any guff from anyone."

"Which didn't endear her to Super," Mrs. Bowman said dryly.

Susan grinned. "Mother used to be a nurse and is good friends with Superintendent Marlow...and with Mrs. Pecker...and with just about everyone else who's anybody at the hospital. I couldn't get away with anything!"

"She didn't get along with Superintendent Marlow, and yet she was at her table for the tea?" Charley asked.

"Truth be told, she didn't get along with any of the oldies particularly well—sorry Mother. But, yes, especially not with Super. That was why we were all so surprised when Super specifically asked Wendy to sit at her table."

"Was that unusual?" Charley turned to Mrs. Bowman.

"It was Super's tea. She set the seating plan. I didn't think that much about it," she said.

"Were they at odds over anything specific?" Mark asked.

"The usual," Susan said. "She didn't think the nurses got enough respect from the doctors and wanted Super to do more about it."

"Any doctor in particular?" Mark asked.

"No, pretty much all of them. The men, anyway. The women doctors are better—mostly."

"What did she think the Superintendent could do?" Mark asked.

"Talk to the Chief about keeping their hands to themselves, to start with." She sounded disgusted. "But it's more than that. We are with the patients all the time. They swoop in and think they know what's best. If we tell them a dose of medication they've prescribed is too much or too little, they refuse to listen. They treat us no better than the janitors. Sometimes they make mistakes. Despite what they think, they are not God!" Susan gasped for breath.

Mrs. Bowman jumped up from her chair and hurried to her daughter. "Relax. Take a deep breath. There now... good." She glared at Charley and Mark. "She is still very weak. Her heart will likely never recover from—"

"Yes, it will!" Susan said fiercely. "I refuse to spend the rest of my life on your sofa."

Mrs. Bowman rolled her eyes and returned to her chair.

"Sorry about that," Susan said. "I tend to get a little emotional when I talk about nursing. We all do."

"But especially Wendy?" Charley prompted.

"Especially Wendy. Most of us put up with poor treatment as part of the job, but not her. She was determined to fight for better, which put her at odds with Super on most days." Susan leaned back and closed her eyes, clearly exhausted.

It was time to go. Charley stood up to leave and paused. "One more thing, if you don't mind," she said.

"I think she's had enough," Mrs. Bowman said.

"It's okay," Susan said, opening her eyes. "I want to help if I can."

"Adeline," Charley said. "She didn't come to the reunion. Do you know why?"

"Adeline Rogers—oops, she's Banks, now." Susan shook her head. "She never fit in, but to be fair, I don't think she tried very hard. We were all a little surprised when she didn't come to the reunion—she does live here, after all. We thought for sure she'd come if only to lord it over us how wonderful it is to be Mrs. Colin Banks. Frankly, though, we were all pretty much relieved when she sent her regrets."

"Did you tell all this to the police?" Mark asked, dodging the evil eye Mrs. Bowman was giving him.

"I never spoke to the police."

7

"Don't you find it odd that the police didn't question Susan Bowman?" Charley had been mulling over the information Susan had given them since they had left the Bowman home. They'd immediately headed to Kingston General Hospital for a conversation with Superintendent Marlow. Not only had she sponsored the tea, but her table had hosted three of the victims, most notably—and surprisingly, according to Susan—Wendy Walker.

"Not necessarily," Mark said, holding open the hospital's door for her. "By the time she was well enough to be questioned, they'd probably already decided that no crime had been committed and had moved on to something else."

"But still..." Charley was baffled. She'd known Constable Marillo for many years and knew he prided himself on being thorough. This seemed like an unlikely loose end to leave hanging.

"Cops are busy," Mark said. "As soon as one case is done, they're on to the next. I don't think you should read anything into it."

Except there had been more incidents. And another death. But Charley kept her thoughts to herself. It was now up to her and Mark to prove a crime or crimes had, indeed, taken place. She was fully convinced; she wasn't so sure about him.

A student nurse pointed the way to Superintendent Marlow's office. The door was closed, and they could hear angry voices—two males and one female—from inside.

"Might as well have a seat and wait it out," Mark said, dropping into one of the folding metal chairs that book-ended the door.

Charley took the chair on the opposite side of the doorway and angled her ear to try to hear what was being said.

"Subtle." Mark grinned at her

"It's no good. Their voices are too muffled." She jumped to her feet and began pacing the hallway.

"Tiger, we've been through this before. You must learn patience. Waiting is part of the game."

Suddenly the door flew open and two white-coated men stormed out. The first—dark-haired with a surly expression —almost knocked over Charley as he marched past. The second, a smaller, rounder blond, paused and apologized for his colleague before swiftly following him down the hallway.

"You okay, Charley?" Mark took her arm.

"Yeah, fine." She glanced toward the doorway where Superintendent Marlow was watching them with concern creasing her brow.

"I'm sorry about that," she said. "Are you here to see me? Please, come in."

Charley took the opportunity to closely examine the woman while Mark made the introductions. Her first impression was that Superintendent Marlow was an imposing presence. She was tall—close to six feet—and certainly broad enough to intimidate most male doctors. Charley's second thought was that Marlow was younger than expected—mid-forties, maybe?—given that she was responsible for the hospital's entire nursing staff. She was dressed in white from head to toe—white cap, belted white dress, white stockings, and white shoes. The colour did nothing to enhance her florid complexion.

"I'm a big fan of yours, Mrs. Hall," she said as a pink stain spread across her freckled cheeks. "I was sorry to see you move from the city beat to the women's pages."

"Thank you. I am hoping it's temporary."

"Amen to that." She smiled.

Yellow teeth.

Charley looked at the woman's hands and saw her fingers were stained with nicotine. Ah, so the stale cigarette smell belonged to her and not one of the doctors who had just left.

"How can I help you? Are you working on a story for the *Tribune*?" Marlow asked. She motioned for them to sit while she rounded her desk and took her seat.

"No. We've been asked to do a bit more digging into the death of Wendy Walker and the other incidents."

Marlow blinked in surprise. "By whom? I thought the police had closed their investigation."

"They have. But given the subsequent illnesses with the Hotel Dieu nurses and then the death of Dr. Young last weekend...well, as you might imagine, some of the nurses and female medical students are wondering if there might be something more going on."

"Hmmm." Marlow bit her lower lip. "I've heard rumblings. I make it my business to know everything that goes on in my hospital. But it's nothing more than idle speculation. There's been nothing to suggest Wendy's death was foul play, was there?"

"No ma'am," Mark said in a brusque, business-like tone. "But if you could answer a couple of questions, we'll be able to square this away, satisfy all concerned, and then we can put it all behind us and move on."

"Well, if there is anything I can do to help my girls, of course, you can count on me," Marlow said.

"Thank you." He reached into his shirt pocket and withdrew a notebook and rifled through a few pages, pretending to read.

What is he playing at?

Charley knew there was nothing related to their investigation in that notebook. It was an act.

"Now, let's see. You were the official host of the tea for the nurses' reunion on the afternoon of August 6, correct?"

Marlow sat up straighter. "Yes."

"And what does that entail?" Mark looked up and gave Marlow a brilliant smile. "Forgive me, I've never been to a tea."

"Well, in this case, it's merely a formality." She looked slightly embarrassed. "The reunion is organized by Mrs. Bowman, and Mrs. Pecker did the actual coordinating of food and drink for the tea—for the whole weekend, actually. The Superintendent's Tea is a long-standing tradition, but it's been many years since the Superintendent has done anything other than show up for it."

"Who arranged the seating?"

"Oh, I did. Sorry, Detective, that is the one responsibility of the Superintendent."

"Quite all right, Superintendent. No harm done, now we know the truth."

Ah, Charley understood now. Marlow was a by-the-book person and by behaving like a police officer on official business, Mark hoped she would feel compelled to respond to his questions. She grudgingly admired how he could quickly size up someone and adapt his interrogation to what he thought would be to the best effect. But in this instance, Charley knew his approach was all wrong.

He glanced down at his notebook. "I understand Wendy Walker and two of the three other women who fell ill were at your table."

"Yes, I'm afraid so."

"Why did you seat Miss Walker at your table?"

"I don't understand..." She seemed taken aback by the question.

"It was well known by all that the two of you didn't get along. It would seem to me, if you were interested in a pleasant afternoon, you'd have avoided placing her at your table."

Marlow's expression hardened and Charley knew Mark had pushed too hard and had reached a dead end in his interrogation. Superintendent Marlow had not risen through the ranks by being pushed around—especially by men. "I don't think I like what you're insinuating."

Mark opened his mouth to reply but Charley stopped him. "I apologize for Detective Spadina," she said ignoring the murderous glare he shot at her. "As he admitted, he's never attended a tea. And as a man, he doesn't understand the subtleties involved in such an event. I suspect you had an important reason for seating Wendy at your table, isn't that right?"

Marlow physically shifted in her chair to angle herself toward Charley and away from Mark. "You are correct, Mrs. Hall." She glanced down at her desk, sighed, and then raised her gaze. "It's no secret there was no love lost between Wendy and me. She was impertinent and outspoken, and a pain in the neck. That's all true. But she was also an amazing nurse—certainly the best in her class, probably the best I've seen in all my years here. She made my life difficult, yes. But what she was after was not wrong. These girls work hard, under difficult circumstances. They deserve to be treated better than they are. They shouldn't have to fight off a doctor's amorous advances with one hand and his disrespectful belittling of her skills with the other."

"Was there anyone in particular she was worried about?"

"A couple of the residents have been especially obnoxious. That was what I was doing when you arrived. I'd received a complaint about another groping incident on the pediatric floor."

"Is it only the residents?"

"If only," Marlow said wistfully. "Unfortunately, some of the doctors believe they have earned the right to behave poorly, too. I can exert some control over the residents and interns, but the doctors...? That is a whole different kettle of fish."

"And so, at the tea...?" Charley prompted.

"I wanted to tell Wendy, away from the hospital, that I admired what she was doing. I appreciated that she was trying to improve things for the girls and I would try to help her in any way I could. I couldn't tell her that here, you understand?"

Charley did. "No, of course not. But in a social setting, it would be perfectly fine to have that conversation."

"Which we did, and then she became ill and had to go lie down."

"What do you think happened?" Charley asked.

"I don't know, but I don't think my girls are wrong to be worried."

Charley nodded. "Too many coincidences. All women. All hospital workers. Always Friday."

"And don't forget Mrs. Pecker," Marlow said. "There's also Geneva Pecker."

After Superintendent Marlow's comment, Charley dearly wanted to visit Geneva Pecker, but she needed to show her face at the *Tribune* if only to remind Sherman she was still around. She made Mark swear to hold off on any more inquiries until the next day, when she would be available again. He agreed but not without finagling a breakfast invitation first.

Honestly, the number of times he'd wrangled breakfast out of her...

Charley reviewed the lineup for this weekend's edition of the women's pages, updated Grace on what she and Mark had learned, and then called Romeo Arcadi to drive her home. It was even hotter than yesterday, and she'd learned her lesson.

She sat in the back seat of Arcadi's cab, rolled down the window, and extended her arm to surf the air currents. She'd noted the baseball bat Arcadi kept beside him for protection. It was from the fifth game of last year's World Series and signed by New York Yankee Joe DiMaggio. The *Trib*'s sports editor had assured her it would more than replace the one he had been forced to hand over to the federal police after using it to come to her defence last month. He'd accepted the gift with unusual humility and then never spoke of it again. He was, however, fond of bringing up the name of his unmarried son, Dominic.

Bessie and Freddie looked up from the cribbage board as she entered the drawing room.

"Good, you're home!" Freddie said. "What did you find out?"

Charley glanced guiltily toward Gran and then threw her brother an exasperated glare. Of course, he had told her. Freddie couldn't keep a secret if his life depended on it.

She shook off her irritation. It didn't matter. The jig would have been up tomorrow morning anyway when Mark arrived for breakfast.

Charley stood in front of one of the two floor fans, enjoying how the cool air wrapped around her body. The room was dim as the curtains had been drawn against the heat. She gave them a summary of her meetings with Susan Bowman and Superintendent Marlow, and what she and Mark planned for tomorrow.

"That's it?" Freddie gaped at her. "I don't understand why you're bothering with those old cases. They happened weeks ago. Why wouldn't you try to find out more about the most recent one?"

"I think the point is to try to find some basis for comparison," Gran interjected. "By starting at the beginning one can move forward and look for common elements—a *modus operandi*, I believe it's called—something that connects all three incidents, and perhaps can help predict when the person or persons will strike next. Isn't that right, Charlotte?"

"Yes, exactly." Charley grinned at her grandmother. "Did you learn that from your latest book club selection?"

"The ladies and I quite enjoyed the novel. In fact, we

are thinking of reading another detective book this month. Do you have any suggestions?"

"I don't usually read detective books," Charley said. "But I've heard Agatha Christie is quite popular."

"Not dark enough, I'm afraid. The ladies want a real gritty murder mystery to sink their teeth into." Her expression suddenly brightened. "Do you think Detective Spadina would be willing to come to our next meeting? It would give them such a thrill to hear from a real detective."

Charley turned to face the fan so her grandmother couldn't see her resentment. *What is wrong with asking me?* She'd been instrumental in solving two recent murders, plus she had years of experience exposing crime on the city beat.

But Charley knew the answer. Bessie did not approve of her granddaughter's involvement in the seamier aspects of being a reporter. She would be much happier if Charley would give up working altogether and, instead, spend her time hosting teas or charity functions as she did. Charley cringed at the thought.

"You can ask Mark tomorrow morning," she said turning back towards her grandmother once she'd managed to force an agreeable expression onto her face. She wondered what his response would be. On the one hand, he was stingy about revealing parts of his past. On the other hand, he was conceited enough to enjoy being the centre of attention.

"I have news," Freddie said, mercifully changing the subject. "I'm returning to university to finish my degree."

"Oh, Freddie, how wonderful." The surge of relief she felt rushing through her surprised Charley. She had spent so long worrying about her brother and now, finally, he seemed to be coming back to them.

"I spoke to the head of the English department and he

says I can pick up from where I left off in '39. I officially registered today and purchased all my books for the first term." He put down the hand of cards he'd been holding. "I think you win again, Gran." He stood, bent to kiss her cheek. "I'm going to get a start on my reading. I'll see you at dinner."

Charley took the chair vacated by her brother. She knew Gran was thinking the same thing. It had only been a few weeks, but maybe this time, Freddie was finally on the road to recovery.

"I am surprised at your interest in crime novels," Charley said.

Bessie's eyebrows rose and she cocked her head to one side. "Haven't I always taken an interest in your pursuits? Perhaps I've finally realized you aren't going to change, and I simply want to know more about what is involved in solving a murder."

"If you can't beat 'em, join 'em?"

"Precisely."

Charley eyed her suspiciously. It wasn't like Gran to admit defeat. She was up to something.

"I think it's good you have an activity that you enjoy. It makes life so much more worthwhile," Bessie added.

Whatever it was, Charley figured Gran would let her know eventually. Until then, however, she was anxious to get out of her damp work clothes and into a cool bathtub. She made her excuses and hurried upstairs to her room.

She could distantly make out the ringing of her personal telephone in her bedroom over the sound of the water filling the tub.

Dan was returning her call. *Finally!*

She turned off the water but didn't rush to answer. Let him stew a bit like he had been making her do for the past few weeks. She knew he was busy with responsibilities for running his family's shipbuilding business as well as serving as a city alderman, but it was unusual for him to be absent from her life for so long. Still, as relieved as she was, she wasn't going to let him off the hook too easily.

She slowed her pace a tad more and let the telephone ring a few more times before she answered.

It wasn't Dan.

It took a few moments for her to register that it was an unfamiliar voice, a woman's, that responded to her "hello."

"I'm sorry to bother you at home," the woman said, "but they gave me this number when I tried to call you at the *Tribune*."

"It's quite all right," Charley said. "I'm sorry I didn't catch your name."

"It's Banks. Adeline Banks and..."

For the second time in as many moments, Charley was caught off guard.

Adeline Banks?

Why was she calling? Had she learned of Charley's investigation? Did she know something about what had happened to her classmates?

What did she say?

"I am sorry, again," Charley said. "Can you repeat that?"

A small pause was followed by a huff of annoyance. "I am calling to invite you to our home for a special announcement we are making Thursday evening. I think it is something your readers will be quite interested in."

"Is this about Wendy Walker and the other girls from your reunion that fell ill?" Charley asked, still trying to get her bearings.

"What? Oh, absolutely not! I don't know anything at all about that."

"Then what is it about?"

"I am not at liberty to say right now, but I promise you, you won't want to miss this. I guarantee it will be the main story on the women's page this weekend."

"Hey, what gives? You've been distracted all morning."

Charley winced as Mark snapped his fingers barely an inch from her face to get her attention. She swatted his hand away. "I'm fine."

"All evidence to the contrary," he said.

She shrugged. She was, what Gran would call, "in a mood." It wasn't even mid-morning and already the temperature had surpassed yesterday's high of 85 degrees. She was hot. She was irritable. And Mark didn't help.

Did he have to be so gosh-darn cheerful? He was never cheerful.

He had positively preened with pleasure when Bessie had asked him to talk to her book club next month. Of course, he had accepted, even recommending a book they might read—one he was particularly fond of. For some reason, Gran was more receptive to Mark's suggestion of Agatha Christie than she had been to Charley's. Maybe it was because it came with an assurance he would be as scandalous as Gran would like when he regaled her book club ladies with stories of his cases.

As exasperated as Charley was with both Gran and Mark, she knew they weren't responsible for her preoccupation.

It was that telephone call from Adeline Banks. Was it a coincidence that she had contacted Charley now? She had denied it had anything to do with their investigation, and yet...?

"Are you ready?" Mark had exited the car, walked around to open her door and was gazing down at her expectantly.

She nodded and joined him on the sidewalk in front of the large rooming house that sat kitty-corner to KGH.

"Superintendent Marlow said I should expect a visit from you," Mrs. Pecker said, ushering them into a sitting room. It was a spacious room and gave off the impression of comfort despite being somewhat shabby. The couches appeared well-worn, and the chairs and end tables formed a mismatched collection of what Charley presumed were hand-me-downs from well-meaning friends and relations.

The woman seemed to have an affection for clocks. There was a large grandfather clock near the entrance and three—no four—mantle and table clocks arrayed throughout this room alone. And the ticking... How did her charges manage? It would drive her crazy if she lived here.

"A cup?" Mrs. Pecker asked, holding up a large Brown Betty teapot. Charley and Mark both declined, and she lowered it, looking disappointed.

Like her sitting room, Geneva Pecker also looked to be a bit worn on the outside. Her clothing was practical, but Charley noted some fraying around the sleeves of her dress. Her age was difficult to determine, but certainly mid-fifties. Her hair had more grey than brown and her eyes were sunk deep into a thin, angular face. Her movements were precise and efficient. Timely, like her clocks.

But also, like her sitting room, Geneva Pecker exuded an aura of warmth and comfort. A safe port in the storm was

Charley's thought. Very appropriate for someone who was housing young women, many of whom were away from home for the first time.

"What did Superintendent Marlow tell you?" Mark asked.

Charley had been surprised that Superintendent Marlow would alert Mrs. Pecker to their visit. She and Mark had both assumed there was some animosity between the two women. Given her remarks, Super seemed to be pointing a finger of blame for what happened directly at Mrs. Pecker.

"Oh, only that you were looking into what happened to my girls. Of course, because it happened here—or at least we assume so—I would fall under suspicion. And of course, none of the girls at my table were affected. But I can assure you, I wouldn't hurt any of them."

"No one is suggesting you would, Mrs. Pecker," Mark said. "There were two other incidents, however, and Superintendent Marlow has tied you to both of those, also."

"It's no secret that Super and I butt heads," Mrs. Pecker said. "She thinks I'm too soft on them and I think she's too hard. But in the end, I truly believe we both want the same thing for our girls."

"Let's start at the beginning. What can you tell us about the day of the tea?" Mark asked.

"We do it every year. The previous year's graduating class comes back for a reunion. It provides inspiration for the current class. That day, I had the nursing students up early, cleaning, and preparing the food for the tea. Simple sandwiches and the like."

"I heard there were pastries, too," Charley said.

"Helloooo?" a high-pitched voice called loudly from the hallway.

"Perfect timing!" Mrs. Pecker jumped to her feet. "We're in here Claire." She turned to Charley. "I asked my sister to join us."

The two sisters could not have been more different physically. Claire Zammit, as she was introduced, was short and round with platinum blonde—presumably dyed—hair. But like Mrs. Pecker, she exuded an open, welcoming demeanor.

"They had just asked about the pastries for the tea," Mrs. Pecker said. "Claire runs a bakery. She's the one who made all the sweets."

"And for the shower at Hotel Dieu. And the weekly Friday get-together for the lady doctors," Claire's voice filled the room.

"And a host of other events and activities not related to either of the hospitals," Mrs. Pecker quickly added.

"How does it work?" Mark asked. "Superintendent Marlow seemed to imply that you, Mrs. Pecker, are the link to all three incidents."

"I guess that's true." She tilted her head thoughtfully. "At least when it comes to the pastries. I take the orders and pass them along to Claire. She gives nurses and doctors a special discount on account of our mum, who was a nurse."

"And our father, who was a doctor," Claire said. "He had his practice right here in this house."

"You have a very strong connection to the medical community in Kingston," Charley said. "But why do the orders have to go through you, Mrs. Pecker? Can't they call Mrs. Zammit directly?"

The two women exchanged amused glances. "They could," Mrs. Pecker replied. "But they are not very well-organized, you understand. I have a strict rule that orders must be given to me by midday Wednesday the week-of. No exceptions. I place my order at 3 p.m. sharp. Super thinks I'm soft. Well, Claire here, is a complete marshmallow. She couldn't say 'no' to a flea."

"Geneva is quite protective of me." Claire smiled affectionately at her sister.

"As an older sister should be," Mrs. Pecker said. "In addition to running the bakery, Claire also looks after our mum, who is not well."

"I'm sorry," Mark and Charley said in unison.

"Was there anything unusual about those three orders?" Mark asked.

Claire shook her head. "Not that I remember."

Mrs. Pecker withdrew several sheets of paper from the sideboard and handed them to Mark. "Here are the orders. You can see for yourself."

"They all wanted *macarons*, of course. They always do. But other than that, the orders were different. *Madeleines*, ginger cakes, *eclairs*. There was a lovely opera cake requested specifically for the shower. I was so pleased with how that turned out. You don't think it was my fancies, do you?"

Charley shook her head. "I don't see how it could be—" Charley began, only to be drowned out by the simultaneous clang of clocks throughout the house, all chiming the hour.

"Does that go on all day and night?" The ticking seemed to have almost disappeared in the deafening silence that followed. Or maybe it was masked by the ringing in her ears.

"Oh, no. I turn them all off at bedtime. I find they help keep the girls on track," Mrs. Pecker said. "You were saying whether you thought Claire's pastries could be responsible."

"All the girls were eating them, so I don't see how they

could be. We're examining everything, trying to find common elements between the three events."

"Of course." Claire looked relieved.

"Did you know the other nurses? The ones from Hotel Dieu?" Charley asked Mrs. Pecker.

"Only a bit."

"And the female medical students?"

"The same. In truth, my only contact with them is to order pastries from Claire."

"What can you tell us about Wendy Walker?" Mark asked. "I hear she was a bit of a handful."

Mrs. Pecker chuckled. "But not a troublemaker. She kept me on my toes, but I've had far worse young ladies in my care."

"What about Adeline Banks?" Charley asked.

Mrs. Pecker looked taken aback by the question. "Adeline, dear Adeline. She wasn't Banks when she was here, of course. Rogers, that was her name. From Sydenham, just outside of town. I knew as soon as she arrived that she was more interested in finding a husband than a career. She had her heart set on a doctor at first, but then she met Mr. Banks and, according to her, 'it was love at first sight'." Mrs. Pecker paused and stared down at her clasped hands. She looked like there was more she wanted to say but was reluctant.

"Anything else?" Charley prompted.

"Well, I guess if you've talked to the others, you'll know she wasn't well-liked by her classmates. But I found her quite charming, though. And I was impressed she stayed until graduation."

"Have you heard from her since then?"

Mrs. Pecker shook her head. "Only a note sending her regrets for the reunion. I was disappointed, but not surprised. It was around the same time as the Liberal leadership convention in Ottawa, and I know Mr. Banks is a supporter of the party. She didn't give me a reason for not joining us, but I am going to assume that was it."

Generous of you.

"What about you, Mrs. Zammit? Did you know her?"

Claire shook her head. "No. Geneva takes in so many young women, I certainly can't remember them all. Heavens, I'm so busy most of the time, I have trouble remembering the names of my regular customers." She chuckled, somewhat embarrassed by the confession.

"Can either of you think of anything that would have caused the type of illness that killed Wendy Walker?" Mark asked.

The sisters looked at each other and shrugged.

"Given our family's involvement in medicine and all we've seen over the years you'd think so, wouldn't you?" Mrs. Pecker said. "But no. Claire and I have talked about this a lot. We've never seen nor heard anything like it."

CHARLEY WANTED to wipe that "I told you so" expression off Mark's face. He had agreed to help investigate as a favour to Laine. He'd never believed a crime had been committed. Now, it seemed he had been proven correct.

"I'm so sorry," Charley said, her eyes darting between Laine and Grace as the four of them sat at a table in Joe's diner. "I was sure, given all the similarities, that there had to be something—or someone—behind what had happened to all those women. The pastries seemed the most obvious culprit given that they were at all three events. But what possible motive would Claire Zammit or Geneva Pecker have?"

"And more importantly, if it had been the pastries, then everyone who ate them should have fallen ill," Grace added. "In terms of motive, I did do some checking to see if I could find any connection between the two women who died." She shook her head. "Aside from the fact that both Wendy Walker and Barbara Young worked at KGH, I came up with nada. But I followed up with the hospital's administrator and it doesn't appear that they ever worked in the same department at the same time. And their backgrounds are completely different. Wendy is from Trenton and Barbara's from Collingwood. One's a nurse, one's a doctor." She slumped down in her chair. "I feel like I've failed you."

Laine squeezed her hand in sympathy. "Maybe there is nothing to find," she said. "It's possible some underlying medical condition caused both Wendy's and Barb's hearts to stop beating." She chewed the inside of her cheek. "It's just with the others presenting with similar symptoms..."

"Not every mystery is a crime," Mark said.

"I feel silly for asking you to look into this but thank you for indulging me."

"Any time, Doc, you know that." Mark stood. "Sorry ladies, I've got an appointment to get to, so I'm going to skedaddle." He glared at Charley as she reached down for her pocketbook. "Don't even think about it. This is on me." He pulled his billfold out of his trouser pocket and sauntered over to the cash register.

"Refill?" Gillian appeared at their table holding up a pair of carafes—coffee and tea. She poured three cups and took away Mark's empty one.

"Maybe Mark is right." Charley hated to admit it. "We talked to everyone who was at the three incidents and there was nothing that the ones who fell ill did that was any different from the ones who didn't. I'm afraid it's back to you, Laine. If there was some specific cause, it has to have been medical—maybe the flu or something like that."

"We'll likely never know," Laine said, adding another heaping teaspoon of sugar to her coffee. Given her addiction to sugar, Charley wondered how she had survived wartime rationing. Grace, on the other hand, was more puritan and liked her tea clear.

Charley took a sip of her coffee—hot, strong, and black. *Perfect.*

"I'd tell you that we'll know for sure if it's a pattern

tomorrow, but to my knowledge, none of the nurses or medical students are planning any sort of get-together that day." Laine kept her eyes downcast as she slowly stirred her cup. "We're all too scared."

"Are you working on Friday?" Charley asked.

"Yeah, I've been doing extra shifts to make up for the time I took off last weekend."

"I never thanked you properly for that." Charley's heart felt full as she gazed at her two friends. "The change in Freddie since you've been sailing together has been nothing short of a miracle. Did you know he's planning to return to school next month?"

"Yes, we talked about it last weekend," Grace said.

"It is still very early in his sobriety," Laine cautioned. "Be watchful, Charley; it wouldn't take much for him to slip again. It's rarely a straight line from addiction to recovery."

Charley reluctantly tempered her enthusiasm. Although she desperately wanted Freddie to return to his old self, she respected Laine's warning. It had only been a couple of weeks. "I'm just happy to see him making progress and so grateful for the two of you."

"And I'm grateful he has a sloop and we can get out on the water, especially if this heat wave continues," Grace said, cooling herself with the paper placemat she had folded into a fan.

Impossibly, today seemed much hotter than yesterday, although the weather prognosticators said there was a one-degree difference—91 compared to 90. But an absence of the fresh, southwest wind that had brought relief yesterday gave free rein to the humidity today. People were doing what they could to stay cool. Some businesses announced they would be closing early, and the beaches and city wading pools were jammed with people of all ages. Charley

67

had seen young children in her neighbourhood cooling themselves off with water from garden hoses. Day seven and no end in sight.

"Lucky you," Laine said miserably. "This heat is becoming dangerous for a lot of elderly people and others who can't get away from it. We're expecting to be deluged by heatstroke victims at the hospital today." She glanced at her watch. "And with that, I need to get back. Thanks again, Charley, for humouring me." She squeezed Grace's shoulder. "And you, you lucky duck, enjoy your sail on the lake."

"You could come with us, Charley," Grace said as the door whooshed closed behind Laine. "Freddie would love it."

"I don't think so." As hot as she was, she couldn't imagine going out in a boat—and certainly not the *Lady Stonebridge*—unless there was a compelling reason to do so.

"Suit yourself. What are you going to do today?"

Charley shrugged. "Work, I guess, and then relax in a cool bath at home." She had originally planned to go to whatever it was that Adeline Banks had invited her to this evening, but with the investigation at a dead end, she no longer saw any reason to. Adeline hadn't even been there, so there was nothing she could say that would shed any more light on what had happened. Besides, the woman's superior attitude and her assumption that she knew what Charley should find newsworthy rubbed her the wrong way. It was no wonder she had not been liked by her classmates. Charley hadn't even met the woman and already she'd left a less than favourable impression.

No, Charley would let Adeline Banks send in her social notice to the *Tribune* as everyone else did. And then she, the editor, would decide if it was worthy to publish in the Saturday edition of the women's pages.

"WELCOME HOME, MRS. HALL," Rachel greeted Charley in the hallway. "Your grandmother has retired to her room and requested a cold plate be brought to her for dinner. Detective Spadina said he would be satisfied with the same, but I could make something different if—"

"Detective Spadina is here?" Charley dropped her satchel beside the hall table and began fanning her face with her hat.

"Yes, he's waiting for you in the drawing room."

"Why?" Seeing the confusion on Rachel's face she shook her head. "Never mind. Yes, a cold plate would be lovely. Thank you."

Mark was standing in front of a fan, and he turned around as Charley entered the room. Her eyes widened in surprise. He was freshly shaved and wearing a crisp, white shirt with a black bow tie, and perfectly creased, black trousers. A white dinner jacket lay over the back of an armchair. "Where are you off to?"

"Don't tell me you've forgotten," he said, feigning disappointment. "I'm crushed."

Charley walked to the sideboard and poured herself a glass of iced tea. She held the glass against her forehead.

She hated it when he toyed with her like this. "I don't know what you're talking about," she snapped.

"Adeline Banks' party, remember?"

"I'm not going to that. What's the point?" She had planned to invite Dan to accompany her, but he hadn't returned her calls. She had forgotten she'd even mentioned it to Mark.

"Don't tell me I'm all dressed up with no place to go. You're breaking my heart, Tiger."

"It's hot. The only thing I want to do is change into something lighter and lie in front of a fan all evening."

Mark turned one of the floor fans so it blew cool air directly on her.

"Thank you," she said grudgingly. "You clean up nicely, by the way. Where'd you get the suit?"

Mark adjusted his bow tie. "Maybe I own it."

She cocked her head and raised her eyebrows skeptically.

"Or maybe I rented it."

"Your appointment earlier today."

"You'd make a great detective, Tiger. Anyone ever tell you that?"

She slumped down in her favourite chair and Mark adjusted the fan toward her again. "Okay, why don't you tell me why you think we should still go to the party," she said. "What can Adeline Banks tell us? We've already determined no one was responsible for what happened."

"Very true. But she is the one person involved to whom we haven't spoken. I do not like loose ends. When I close an investigation, I like to make certain nothing has been overlooked."

She took a long sip of her iced tea. She didn't want to go out in this heat again.

"C'mon, Tiger. What is the harm? Put on your glad rags and let's have a little fun. At the very least, the food's bound to be good. What do they call those tiny nibble-sized things?"

"*Canapés*, I think you mean."

Honestly, does that man ever think of anything other than food?

He did have a point, though. She didn't like loose ends, either. And despite her irritation with Adeline Banks, she was curious to meet this woman whom the rest of her classmates had such little regard for. Charley couldn't help but wonder if she truly deserved her reputation or if it was sour grapes because she'd snagged a rich husband.

Charley asked Rachel to serve dinner in the drawing room as it was cooler than the dining room.

"How is Gran?" she asked as Rachel arranged their plates on the coffee table.

"I'm encouraging her to drink more water than tea, but she's—" Rachel stopped suddenly and her face flushed pink.

"Stubborn, I know," Charley grinned. "It's okay to say it. Even she wouldn't dispute you."

Rachel finished her preparations and hurried from the room.

Mark sat down on the couch and began piling his plate with an assortment of cold meats and fruit. "I like Rachel. She has a good head on her shoulders," he said, picking up a cube of cheese and popping it into his mouth.

Charley returned to her chair with her plate.

Do not ask him. Don't do it.

But her curiosity got the better of her. "So, have you been able to ferret out all her secrets, Detective? Do you know where she's from? What she did before she came to work for us?"

"I was going to ask you. It's your family she works for."

Charley poked at her salad. "She doesn't offer a lot of information and Gran has forbidden me from questioning her," she admitted, spearing a tomato.

"That's too bad."

She looked up sharply and he avoided her gaze. "You haven't been able to get anything out of her either, have you?" She chuckled. "You must be losing your touch, Detective. First Superintendent Marlow and now Rachel Winters."

"What are you talking about? We got what we needed from Marlow."

"Oh, come on. You almost blew it with your tough-cop routine. If it hadn't been for me, she'd have clammed up and we'd have had nothing. We never would have found out about Mrs. Pecker and her sister."

"My dear Mrs. Hall, do you know nothing about police interrogation tactics?" His voice dripped with sarcasm.

"Oh, so it was a tactic to have her stop answering your questions?"

"Precisely." He returned his focus to his dinner plate.

She waited, but he showed no indication that he intended to elaborate. She sighed, exasperated. "Okay, explain it to me, Mr. Former-Big-City-Police-Officer."

He gave her that grin she found so disconcerting. Cleaned up and relaxed, he would almost be called attractive—someone she wouldn't mind spending time with.

Too bad this wasn't his normal demeanour. She would do well to keep that uppermost in her mind tonight.

"It's called 'good cop/bad cop'," he said.

"Let me guess. You're the bad cop?"

"Of course. I become aggressive and make the suspect feel uncomfortable, unsafe. And you—"

"Good cop."

"—are sympathetic and understanding. The suspect sees you as a friend, someone who is concerned with their well-being."

"And someone they are comfortable spilling the goods to."

"You're catching on." He winked.

"You're not suggesting we play good cop/bad cop with Rachel, are you?"

Mark seemed taken aback by the suggestion. "No, I doubt it would work on her." He cocked his head. "Unless you think she's deliberately hiding something from us."

Charley shrugged. "She doesn't strike me as the typical domestic. She is obviously well-educated, but it's likely she's fallen on hard times and has to take on this type of work to make ends meet. It's probably pride that makes her reluctant to talk about it."

"Then let's let her keep that to herself."

Charley agreed but was surprised, once again, by the hardened ex-cop's capacity to empathize with others.

"I SHOULD HAVE BROUGHT MY GUN," Mark whispered in her ear as they entered the Bankses' limestone mansion.

Charley flushed at the compliment. It wasn't the first he'd given her since she descended the stairs, dressed in her jade-green, off-the-shoulder evening gown. She had kept her shoulder-length hair loose. There wasn't much else she could do with it in this humidity—at least not in the twenty minutes he'd given her to get ready. She'd completed her look with a pair of jade earrings and the matching pendant; they'd been her father's wedding gift to her mother. The deep green of her gown brought out the iridescent green of her eyes, and the jewellery contrasted with the pale skin of her *décolleté* and drew the eye down to the gentle swell of her breasts. She knew she looked good and the appreciative scrutiny by the men in the room as they entered confirmed Mark's crude whistle of approval when he first saw her.

She didn't know what Adeline Banks had been expecting when she'd invited a newspaper editor to attend her party, but from the look on her face when Charley introduced herself, it wasn't what she got. She had probably been envisioning a frumpy, grey-haired spinster in tweed, Charley thought, conjuring an image of Mildred Preston, her predecessor.

But Charley had grown up in this milieu. If anyone was a stranger to it, it was Adeline, although given how quickly she recovered from her initial fluster, the young woman was learning fast.

It was how well Mark seemed to be fitting in that surprised Charley most. She introduced him and then allowed him to dominate the conversation while she examined their hostess.

If Adeline Banks had been surprised by Charley's appearance, Charley was equally surprised by hers. Perhaps given all the talk by the nurses about how she had attracted a rich husband, she'd expected the woman to be some sort of *femme fatale*. But nothing could be further from the truth. Adeline Banks wasn't especially attractive at all. She was tall, almost as tall as Charley, but stocky. Her hair was an unnatural blonde and she wore a tad too much makeup in a mistaken attempt to cover an overabundance of freckles. Her clothing, however, was impeccable, and it would take someone well-versed in style to realize that the warm brown of her gown was chosen to mask the ruddy hue of her skin, and its cut and shape designed to minimize her height and girth. Only the long sleeves on such a hot day seemed out of place.

But there was something about her...

Charley watched, mesmerized, as Mark, a hard-boiled detective, basked in her attention. Was it her deep blue eyes —her finest feature—that seemed to cast a spell, or the soft, lilting laugh that drew you in as if you shared a secret? Adeline's attention was diverted as she went to greet more arriving guests, and Mark and Charley made their way into a ballroom.

Whatever they were announcing, the Bankses had

pulled out all the stops. Floor-to-ceiling windows were open, each one containing a large fan, pushing the cooler, nighttime air into the room. Lights were kept low to help combat the heat. In the corner, a string quartet was playing Debussy. Two waiters immediately appeared at their side, one offering glasses of champagne and the other, the small *canapés* Mark had been looking forward to. Charley's eyes widened as she watched him shovel four onto a napkin. They both declined the alcohol.

"They will come back you know," she said softly, chastising his poor manners. "They become like mosquitoes you can't get rid of, especially as the evening goes on and the hostess realizes she's over-ordered on the food."

"Charlotte?"

Charley whirled around and recognized Rose Cannon halfway across the room, beetling toward her. She could have sworn she heard Mark mutter an obscenity under his breath.

"I didn't expect to see you here." Rose sounded unusually flustered.

Charley peered at Dan's mother. Her colour was high, but that was likely due to the heat. Her cornflower-blue eyes darted over to Mark. "Good evening, Detective. It's nice to see you again."

"Mrs. Cannon, a pleasure," he said in a voice devoid of emotion.

"I'm here for the *Trib*," Charley explained. "Are you friends of the Bankses?" Seeing Rose here was a big surprise. The Cannons moved in the same social circle as the Stormonts. It was strange that Rose would be invited to what had been touted as a major social event, but not Bessie.

"No, not really," she said looking around nervously. "Daniel is. He and Colin Banks are members of the party."

"The Liberal Party," Charley said for Mark's benefit. "Is Dan here, then? I've been trying to reach him for days—weeks, in fact."

"Hmmm, he has been quite busy, especially since the convention. What did you say you were doing here, Charlotte? Something for the paper? What about you, Detective?"

"He's here for the *canapés*," Charley said as Mark stepped away to follow another of the drifting waiters. She knew his real intention was to get away from Rose before she could pigeonhole him into agreeing to come for tea and a chat about his childhood.

"Charley! What are you doing here?" Dan appeared beside his mother, his face bright red.

"That seems to be a popular question," she snapped. "Why wouldn't I be here?" The sudden appearance of Dan after so many weeks should have made her happy, but instead, she felt annoyance and she wanted to lash out at him. "What about you? You're looking quite flushed. Have you been dancing? You should know better in this heat."

"No, I haven't been dancing." He glanced toward Rose. "Did you know she was coming?"

"No, I had no idea."

"Well, hello there, Sport. Fancy meeting you here." Mark had returned to the group holding a napkin piled with an assortment of tiny treats. He popped one into his mouth and then held out the napkin. "Anyone want one? I'm willing to share?" He sidled up beside Charley, unmistakably asserting himself as her date for the evening. "Well, some things, at least."

She didn't think it was possible, but Dan's face seemed

to glow even redder. He took a step toward Mark, fists clenched. They stood inches apart, each trying to out-menace the other. Charley knew she should do something but was frozen to her spot.

"Not here!" Rose's voice was low but firm—a mother's voice that brooked no dissent. Both men took a step back but kept a wary gaze on the other.

Finally, Dan broke away and looked at Charley. "Can we talk?"

"Look, Sport, if you wanted to talk to her you should have returned her telephone calls. That's not too much to ask, is it?"

"I'm not talking to you!" Dan replied to Mark but kept his eyes on Charley's face. "Please, it's important."

"I think you—" Rose began, but Charley held up her hand to stop her from saying anything more.

"Mark is right. If you wanted to talk to me, you should have returned at least one of the dozen or so calls I made over the past month. I'm here with him tonight. You can call me later, and we'll see if I want to talk to you then." She knew she was being petty, but she was deeply hurt by Dan's unexplained abandonment of her. That he had chosen to come here tonight, without her, was another blow.

"Oh, there you are, Daniel." Adeline placed a hand on his back. "It's time."

"But..." Dan looked frantically from Adeline to Rose, to Charley.

"I am so glad you are here, Mrs. Hall. This is going to be the scoop of the year for your newspaper," she said, pulling Dan away.

"Oh, dear, I should be there, too," Rose said. She clenched Charley's arm. "Come and find me afterward. Promise?" Then she was gone.

"So, what do you think the big announcement is?" Mark asked, dropping another *canapé* into his mouth.

She shrugged. "Rose said Dan and Colin are both members of the Liberal party. I know Dan has plans to run in the next election, whenever it's called. Maybe he's formally announcing his candidacy."

"But that would be a political story, wouldn't it? Not one for the women's pages."

Charley knew Mark was correct, but she didn't have time to fully consider the implications. There was a banging of a gong and everyone fell silent. All eyes turned toward the centre of the room where a short, round man with a few wisps of blond hair stood. He introduced himself as Colin Banks, then introduced his wife, Adeline, and thanked everyone for coming.

Upon closer inspection, she realized that Banks had the soft, unwrinkled features of a man who couldn't be much more than thirty. He spoke with a cadence she couldn't place. It bothered her because she generally had a good ear for accents. Maybe it was the heat or the ambiance of the room, but everything seemed to meld together, and Charley found herself getting lost in the rhythm of Banks' unusual speech pattern rather than the message he was delivering.

Suddenly Dan was standing beside him, holding the hand of a slip of a girl, likely Banks' sister, given her pale complexion and blonde—almost white—hair colour. And then there was applause and catcalls and whistles.

"Mother of God!" Mark snarled from beside her. She felt his arm slip around her waist and apply pressure as he urged her to move. "Let's get out of here."

"No, wait." She turned to Mark. There was a vein pulsing at his temple and his dark brown eyes had turned black. "I don't understand..."

The words Colin Banks had said were slowly making their way into her consciousness.

Dan Cannon.

Meredith Banks.

Engagement.

CHARLEY FELT the pressure of a cool, damp cloth being pressed against her forehead. She could hear hushed voices —a man and a woman arguing, and another woman, closer, shushing them.

She raised her hand to remove the cloth and stared into the ocean-blue eyes of Adeline Banks.

"Good, you're awake," she said. "No, don't rush. Take it slowly." She reached around Charley's shoulders and helped her sit up.

While Mark hurried to her side, Rose held back.

"How are you feeling?" His voice was anxious.

She looked around the room—floor-to-ceiling bookcases, a desk, and a collection of wingback chairs, as well as the sofa she was sitting on. "What happened?" Charley asked.

"You fainted," Adeline said. "It must have been the heat."

No, it wasn't the heat. A wave of humiliation was immediately subsumed by the deep loathing for the hostess that arose in her chest. Did she know? Was that why she had insisted Charley, herself, come? "I don't faint."

"This weather's been a trial on everyone." She handed Charley a glass. "Here, have a sip of water."

The door was flung open, making a loud thud against

the wall as Dan rushed into the room. Mark wheeled around and blocked him from approaching Charley.

"Get out of my way," Dan growled.

Mark planted his feet and squared his shoulders. "Make me."

Dan raised his fist to take a swing, but Rose moved quickly to grab his arm. "Not here. Not now." Again, she had managed to diffuse the imminent explosion of violence between the two men.

Dan lowered his arm and took a step back. "Charley?" he called plaintively.

"Do you two know each other?" Adeline stood and glanced between the two.

Maybe she doesn't know.

Charley raised her head to look at Dan. He certainly knew. Let him be the one to explain.

"Daniel?" Meredith Banks' pale grey eyes were as large as saucers as she hesitated in the doorway. She looked ethereal in a simple, silver, satin gown, her long hair hanging loose around her shoulders. She wore no jewellery aside from...

Charley's gaze flew to Meredith's hand. Yes, there it was: the Cannon ruby. Dan had shown it to her one of the times he had asked Charley to marry him.

And now he had given it to someone else.

How could he?

But she knew the answer. He needed a wife. He had made no secret of the fact that his political aspirations demanded it.

But this child? How old was she?

"You must be Charley," Meredith said, seeming to float into the room. She ignored both Dan and Mark, neither of whom seemed capable of moving, and stopped mere inches from the sofa. "I'm so sorry. We didn't know you'd be here. This must come as a terrible shock to you." Her voice was gentle and melodic. It made Charley wonder whether the Banks family had some sort of voice magic—Colin, mesmerizing; his sister, angelic.

Dan jostled Mark out of the way and joined Meredith, but he seemed incapable of speaking.

Adeline placed her hands on her hips. "Well, someone needs to tell me what's going on."

"This is Charlotte Stormont," Meredith said. "Dan's great, childhood friend."

"Stormont," Adeline said, clearly recognizing the name. "I had no idea." Then an ugly swath of red rose from her neck and stained her cheeks as embarrassment took hold. She whirled on Charley. "You never said anything."

Oh, no. You are not going to turn this on me.

Anger burned and she latched onto it for strength. She stood, praying her legs wouldn't betray her. They held. "And you refused to tell me the reason you wanted the *Tribune* to come to your event," she said, summoning as much disdain as she could manage.

"I can't believe you contacted the newspaper, Addie." Meredith sounded disappointed. "We told you we didn't want this. We were only expecting a few people—close friends and family for the time being."

"Obviously, not *all* your close friends." Charley took some satisfaction in seeing Dan blanch at her criticism. The distress in Meredith's eyes bothered her, though. She didn't want to feel anything for the waif, but she couldn't help it. Meredith seemed as bewildered by what had transpired as she did.

"I was going to tell you," Dan said. "I just didn't know how."

"Perhaps if you'd bothered to return any of my telephone calls...oh, never mind." She had already made that argument to him. She walked over to Rose. "I am disappointed in you, though. You should have said something."

"Water under the bridge!" Mark proclaimed in an unusually jovial tone, drawing everyone's attention. "Meredith, we haven't met but let me join Rose, here, in welcoming you to our family." He stepped toward her, held out his hand as if to shake hers, but dropped it and leaned in to kiss her cheek, instead. "I've always wanted a little sister."

"What are you talking about?" Dan yelled.

Charley didn't think Dan could grow any paler but seeing his arch-enemy kissing his *fiancée* seemed to drain the last bit of blood from his face. He wavered slightly and she thought perhaps *he* was about to faint.

"No, not now!" Rose pleaded with Mark.

"Why not now? It seems as good a time as any." He flashed Rose a dazzling smile. The effect was more menacing than his usual scowl. Then he turned back to Meredith and Dan. "Don't worry, Angel. Sport here hasn't been keeping you in the dark like he has Charley; he didn't know."

Dan seemed to recover from his initial shock and grunted with disgust. He took Meredith's arm and attempted to lead her away.

She shook him off. "Know what?" she asked.

"Sport, here, is my baby brother—well, half-brother, actually. Different fathers, same mother."

"You're lying!" Dan lunged at him, but Mark easily sidestepped his attack.

"Ask Rose; she's known for months." He returned his focus back to Meredith. "It's a long and rather sordid tale, but now that you're family—"

Dan's fist made direct contact with Mark's cheek. Mark wheeled backward, crashing into one of the cases and sending a cascade of books to the floor. He staggered forward, fist raised, but Meredith leapt between them.

"Enough!" She glowered at the two men. "Hasn't there been enough hurt and misunderstanding for one evening?" She sniffed and wiped the back of her hand across her cheek, brushing away the tears. "This is supposed to be the happiest time of m-my l-life." She turned and raced from the room.

Dan looked guiltily at the door but did not follow.

Adeline threw him a withering stare and then expelled a breath of pure contempt before going after Meredith.

His shoulders slumped in defeat, Dan turned toward Charley. "I—"

"Don't say anything," she said. She blinked at the stinging tears she had so far managed to keep at bay. She turned to Mark. "I'd like you to take me home now."

"You're still here?" Charley was surprised to see Bessie at the breakfast table a good hour after she'd usually finished.

"Were you hoping to avoid me?"

Charley shook her head. That hadn't been her intention. She'd had a very slow start to her morning after an almost sleepless night.

"You know, don't you?" Charley eyed the fresh fruit and buttered toast, but she had no appetite. She picked up the coffee urn and carried it around to her seat.

"Rose called me first thing this morning."

"You didn't know before?"

"My darling, if I had known, I most certainly would have told you." Bessie frowned. "Rose Cannon has disappointed me many times over the years, but I think this is her greatest transgression. I don't think I shall ever be able to forgive her for it."

"To be fair, Gran, it was Dan's news. He should have been the one to tell me."

It wasn't as if he was betraying her in any way. She'd made it clear she couldn't marry him, not while Theo's fate remained a mystery. Dan had argued that Theo had been missing, presumed killed in action, for six years and now, two years after the end of the war, no one would have criticized her for moving on. She knew he was right. And yet, time and again she had rejected his proposals.

Last night had been awful. After Mark had dropped her off, Charley had gone up to bed, but her thoughts swirled in her mind like a tornado. She was heartbroken that Dan hadn't told her of his plans to marry. Weren't they supposed to be best friends? Why would he keep that a secret from her? Why wouldn't he have invited her, himself, to his engagement announcement?

Close friends and family, Meredith had said.

But as the night wore on and sleep continued to evade her, Charley was forced to face the truth. She had assumed Dan would wait for her.

"What is she like?" Gran asked.

Charley sipped her coffee and considered the question. She wanted to hate Meredith Banks but she couldn't. If anything, she'd been impressed by the young woman's poise last evening. She'd seemed genuinely distressed upon learning of Charley's predicament and had called out Adeline for not heeding her wishes about the party. Then she'd risked grievous personal injury by intervening in the fight between Dan and Mark—not even Rose had dared to step in once the fists had started flying.

Charley felt bad for Meredith. She did not deserve any of the drama and upset that had ruined her engagement party. *This is supposed to be the happiest time of my life.* Charley's heart clenched as she remembered the pain in Meredith's voice when she'd rebuked them all for their boorish behaviour.

"I like her," Charley said, making up her mind. "I think she'll make a good politician's wife."

"Banks, I believe Rose said. I don't know them." Bessie's brow furrowed.

"That's a surprise, I thought you knew everyone."

"I do, but I've never heard of them. Maybe they're new to town."

"I don't know but judging by their home, they have money. And Meredith's brother, Colin, is connected to the Liberal party in some way."

"Ah, well, I guess that explains it all, doesn't it?"

"What does it explain?" Charley asked. "Are you saying Dan's marrying her for her money?"

"And her connections, of course." Gran gave her a piercing stare. "Well, you don't think he's in love with her, do you?"

Charley shifted uncomfortably. She did not want to think about whether he was or not. It shouldn't matter to her, anyway. Not anymore.

"The Cannons' shipbuilding company hasn't recovered as quickly from the last war as it did the previous one," Gran said. "Ted Cannon is returning from Europe any day now, and I've been told the trip wasn't as successful as he'd hoped in terms of getting new contracts."

Charley eyed her grandmother. How did she know all this? Dan had told her the family was facing some financial hardship, but he'd downplayed its severity and insisted it was temporary.

"And it's no secret Daniel plans to run in the next federal election. That's not an inexpensive undertaking."

"I think you're wrong," Charley said, irritated by her compassion for Meredith. "I can't imagine Dan marrying someone solely for her money."

Bessie sighed heavily. "My darling Charlotte, a man's

feelings toward a woman do not change overnight, especially when he's been carrying a torch for her for years. It was merely a few weeks ago that he was trying to persuade you to marry him, despite how unsuitable you are to be a politician's wife. I don't believe for a second he met and fell wildly in love with someone else—someone who just happens to have the funds and connections to aid his political career."

Charley nodded. That made some sense. And then: "Wait a minute! What do you mean I'm 'totally unsuitable' to be a politician's wife?"

Gran cocked her head and raised her eyebrows. "Where do you want me to begin, *Mrs. Hall*? With your job? Your outspoken nature? With—"

"Okay, I get it." Charley held up her hands in defence. "Tact and subtlety aren't my strengths."

"Do tell," Bessie said dryly.

Charley took a final sip of her coffee. "Well, on that note, I need to get to the office."

"You're not going into the *Tribune* today, are you? You've had a terrible shock. Why don't you stay home? I'm having my bridge group over later. You can join us. Play a few hands. It will take your mind off things."

Bridge?

"Thank you, but no. I am going in. It's Friday. I must get tomorrow's women's pages finished. Besides, I hear there's a huge scoop—something about the engagement of a certain city alderman."

"Charlotte, are you certain?" Gran's eyes reflected concern. "I'm sure John Sherman can find someone else to edit the page this one time."

She bent and kissed Bessie's cheek. "I am fine, Gran. Thank you for worrying, but work is the best thing for me right now. Besides, you wanted to know more about the Banks family, didn't you? I'll put my top researcher on it."

She would also ask Grace to call Adeline for a picture of the happy couple—she had no doubt a formal photograph had already been taken. Despite how painful she found it, Charley would put on a brave face and write the article about Dan's engagement to Meredith Banks. He deserved that. But dealing with Adeline again? That would be going above and beyond what she was willing to endure.

Charley retrieved her hat and satchel and was debating whether to walk to work or call a cab. The forecast was for another hot, humid day but it was still early enough that walking wasn't out of the question. Almost simultaneously the hallway telephone rang and there was a knock at the front door. Rachel raced out from the dining room, a panicked expression on her face as her gaze darted back and forth between the ringing telephone and the increasingly insistent knocking.

"I'll get the door, you answer the phone," Charley suggested.

Rachel gave her a grateful nod and went to answer the telephone.

Charley opened the door and her eyes widened in surprise. The young man standing on the doorstep was one of the medical students who'd raced out of Superintendent Marlow's office when she and Mark were there—the rude, dark-haired one who'd almost bowled her over.

"Delivery," he said, holding out a square, white box tied up with pink ribbon.

"Deliveries are made around the side," Charley said but took the box anyway. She glanced at the cursive black letters printed across the top: *Zammit's Fine Pastry Shoppe.*

"Wait!" she called out, but he'd already hopped back into his vehicle.

Charley closed the door and backed into the foyer, staring down at the box.

"The telephone is for you, Mrs. Hall," Rachel called from halfway up the staircase. "I need to wake Mr. Freddie right away."

Charley placed the box on the hallway table and picked up the telephone's handset, more confused than ever. Since she'd had her personal line installed, she rarely received calls at the house number.

"Hello?"

"Ch-Charley? Th-thank goodness...h-h-hoping you were st-still there." Grace was breathless. "It's Laine...h-h-hospital...p-please hurry!"

Charley was quite sure parking the car in front of the door to the hospital was illegal, but she wasn't about to tell Freddie so. They were both anxious to get inside and find out what had happened to Laine.

Oh, please, not the same as Wendy Walker and Barbara Young!

But she was a woman.

She worked in a hospital.

It was Friday.

In the few moments it had taken Freddie to get dressed, she'd arranged for Mildred Preston to finish tomorrow's women's pages. The former editor had been thrilled—apparently, retirement wasn't all she'd hoped it would be. Charley pocketed that piece of intelligence; it might come in handy some time.

Mark, sporting an impressive bruise on his cheek and a black eye, was with Grace. "It's not what you're thinking," he said quickly. "She was attacked."

"They f-f-ound h-h-her...oh, I can't." Grace turned away and Freddie immediately wrapped his arms around their friend and held her close.

"It's okay, Doll. I've got this," Mark said quietly.

Charley had never seen Mark look so shaken up. And

that scared her almost as much as learning that Laine had been beaten.

"She was found unconscious in the lunch room the nurses use," he said.

"Who found her?" Charley asked.

"One of the medical residents. It was about 9:45. She wasn't breathing."

Although muffled by Freddie's shoulder, Grace's wail of despair cut through Charley's heart like a serrated knife. Her emotions were all over the place. She was devastated. She was furious.

"Where is she now?"

Mark shrugged. "Wherever they take people who need to be fixed up. Grace is listed as her next of kin, but she hasn't had any news other than Laine is still alive."

"Police?"

"They're already here. I saw Marillo heading off with one of the white coats when I first arrived."

"So now what?"

"We wait. And we pray." He took Charley's arm and directed her toward the brown Naugahyde couch. He motioned for Freddie to follow them. "Take a seat. This could be a while."

The waiting seemed to stretch on forever. Charley tried to stay still, but she couldn't. She would sit quietly for a bit and then her nerves would turn edgy, her skin crawling for movement. She'd pace around the waiting room and up and down the corridor, offer to get coffee or food—anything to feel like she was doing something—and then return to her seat on the couch, or one of the hard plastic chairs for variety, to try to sit quietly for a while longer.

After the third time she'd gone through this routine,

Freddie reached out and put a hand on her knee to try to calm her.

"How can you just sit here like this?" she asked him. She knew Mark had developed the skill as a cop. Patience was a big part of the job, he had told her. And Grace, never one to draw attention to herself, was curled into a ball at the end of the couch as if she thought that making herself small would hide her from misfortune.

"When you're locked up for years, you learn to be very still," Freddie said quietly.

Charley could hear the anguish in his voice. It was the first time he had referenced what had happened to him after Dieppe. Was it an opening? She glanced at him, but his eyes were downcast, maybe remembering, maybe praying. She took the small morsel as hope that someday soon he would be ready to share it with her.

She heard heavy footsteps and her gaze flew to the entrance of the waiting area. Constable Marillo approached them. She caught his sympathetic glance before he turned to Grace.

"I'm very sorry, Miss Fletcher, but we need to ask you a few questions," he said.

Grace looked up, her pale blue eyes tormented. She unfurled from her ball and held out her hand to Freddie.

"Can I be with her when you question her?" he asked.

"She's not being interrogated and we're not taking her anywhere," Marillo said. "You can all stay where you are." He pulled up a chair and sat down so he could be at eye level with her.

"Do you have any news about Laine?" Grace asked.

"I'm afraid not." He took a deep breath. "Can you think of anyone who would want to hurt her? Has she mentioned any conflicts she's had with patients or co-workers recently?"

"No." Grace shook her head vehemently. "Everyone loved her."

"What about outside the hospital? Boyfriend? Anyone?

Grace hesitated and eyed the constable as if she was trying to decide what she could say. In the end, she mumbled, "She has no boyfriend and there haven't been any conflicts with our friends."

"We're all done," Constable Adams called from the door.

Marillo nodded and stood. He turned back to Grace. "If you think of anything, call the station."

Charley glanced at Mark and leapt to her feet. "Can we see the lunch room?"

Marillo's eyes widened and then he shook his head. "Please, Mrs. Hall, focus on your friends and leave the investigation to us."

She waited until the two officers had left the room before rounding on Mark. "I think we should check it out."

Mark stood. "I do, too. But I'm not sure they'll let us."

"Grace," Charley said gently. "Do you know any of the nurses or medical students here?"

"Of course," she said, colour coming back to her cheeks. She stood up. "I'll go get someone."

"What do you think you're going to find?" Freddie asked.

"I don't know, but I can't just sit here waiting."

Within minutes Grace returned with a young, dark-haired woman in a nurse's uniform whom she introduced as Clara Ross.

"Sure, I can show you the lunch room," she said. "It's a

real mess, though," she added lowering her voice, but Grace heard her anyway and stifled a moan with her hand.

"So, it hasn't been disturbed?" Mark asked.

"No, the police just finished there. But we should hurry; I'm sure the administrator wants it cleaned up pronto."

Clara Ross hadn't been exaggerating. Three of the four chairs were upended and scattered around the room. The fourth was trapped between a square Formica table and the wall. On the other side of the room was a long counter with a sink and cooktop; plates and cups were strewn along the top. As she took a step into the room and looked around, Charley put her hand over her mouth to stifle her gag. So much blood. There was a large pool of it on the floor and splatters of it on the walls.

"The person who did this had to have been covered in blood, too," Mark said. "Was there a blood trail from the room?"

"Yes, all down the corridor," Clara said. She had not entered the room with them but remained standing in the hallway. "It was cleaned up right after the police arrived. Too distressing for the patients."

"Do you know who found her?" Charley asked.

"Dr. Wells. Mitch Wells. He's a resident here."

"What was he doing in the nurses' lunch room?" Charley asked.

"He was setting up for break time. That's around ten. Usually one of the nurses comes in to make coffee, but he was being punished by Super, so..." She shrugged.

Charley remembered the tongue-lashing she and Mark had overheard while they waited to speak with Superintendent Marlow earlier in the week. She could well imagine what the resident was atoning for.

"Do you have any idea how long Dr. Black had been there before she was found?" Mark asked.

"No, I'm sorry. I only know what I've been told."

"Is it common for doctors to go into the nurses' lunch room?" Charley asked.

"It's not all that unusual," Clara said. "That's where the freshest coffee usually is."

"If you hear anything, anything at all, will you please let us know?" Charley said. She knew hospital staff would be more unreserved among themselves than when speaking to the police.

Charley and Mark backed out of the room, careful to retrace their steps so as not to disturb the scene—more out of habit than need since the police had finished with it.

"Is Constable Adams still here?" a student nurse approached.

"The police have left. Why?" Clara asked her.

"I was told to give him this." She held up a small glass jar. "I guess I'll call the station and have someone come get it." She turned to leave.

"Can we see that?" With Mark's authoritative tone, the nurse handed him the jar without question. He held the glass up to the light and peered into it. "What is this?"

The nurse shrugged. "I don't know if it's significant or not, but I was told to give it to the police. Dr. Black was clutching it in her hand when she was found."

Mark shook his head and gave it to Charley. "Any idea?"

Inside was a small, red berry, coated with several yellowish crumbs. She shook the jar gently to get a better look.

Her breath caught in her throat and her hand began to tremble. Mark quickly took the jar from her.

"What is it?" he asked. "A berry of some sort?"

She gazed up at him, the recognition of what she saw turning to horror as its implication became clear. She knew precisely what it was. Although it was referred to as a berry, it was, in fact, a fleshy cone with the purpose of protecting its seed. A seed that was deadly.

CHARLEY TURNED TO CLARA. "Are there usually pastries at your breaks?"

"No, but it's funny you should ask. Dr. Wells wasn't the only one being punished. Dr. Maloney—Brett Maloney—was, too. Super had ordered him to bring in pastries for the nurses."

"That's a strange punishment, isn't it?" Charley asked.

"Well, it's because he does deliveries for Mrs. Zammit's bakery on Fridays. We were all pretty excited about it." She looked thoughtful. "Maybe that was why Dr. Black was here, although I can't imagine her nipping a pastry meant for the nurses. I might expect it from some of the other doctors, but not her."

"I don't remember seeing a pastry box in the lunch room, do you?" Charley asked Mark.

Mark shook his head. "What would it look like?"

But Charley knew exactly what it looked like. Brett Maloney had delivered one to her home earlier this morning. She turned on her heel and ran back to the waiting room.

"What's up?" Mark said, trotting beside her.

"Where's Freddie?" she asked, looking around the empty room.

"And Grace?" Mark added.

Charley hurried over to a telephone box, fishing for a coin from her pocket. She tapped her foot impatiently as the phone rang and rang, but there was no answer.

Dammit!

She slammed down the receiver as Grace shuffled back into the waiting room and slumped down in a chair.

"Do you have news?" Mark asked her.

She nodded and then her face crumpled in anguish.

Charley's heart contracted sharply. *Oh no, not Laine.*

She looked around frantically. She had to get home, but she couldn't leave Grace at a time like this.

Where was Freddie?

"It doesn't look good," Grace said, sobbing into Mark's shoulder. "She's still unconscious and they've had to put her on a mechanical lung."

At least she is still alive.

"Grace," she said gently touching her friend's shoulder. "I need to go home. It's an emergency. I don't want to leave you, but..."

Grace pushed away from Mark and gave Charley a brave smile. "It's fine. They say I can, maybe, see her in a bit —once they've got her settled in a room."

"I'll stay with her," Clara said, sitting down beside Grace. "She's one of us. There are lots of us here who will keep an eye on her to make sure she's okay."

❦

"Do you want to tell me what's going on?" Mark asked as he applied a heavier foot to the gas at Charley's urging.

"It's the pastries," she said, glancing out the window and

noting that Freddie's car was gone from the front of the hospital.

"I thought we ruled those out."

"We did, and I don't know how it works, but Laine must have figured it out. Maybe that was why she was in the lunch room."

"The berry?" he asked.

She nodded. The red fruit surrounded by crumbs meant that the berry must somehow have been in the pastry, but whether it had been added by Claire Zammit or Brett Maloney, she wasn't sure. All she knew was that a box of Zammit's Fine Pastries had been delivered to her home and her grandmother was planning on serving them to her bridge ladies.

"So, it's a poisonous berry?" Mark asked.

"It's not the berry part that's poisonous. You can eat them—they're quite tasty. It's the seed inside that's—"

"You've eaten these berries?"

"As long as you don't eat the seed, you're okay," Charley said. "Or eat the nettles or the bark or any other part of the plant, essentially. It's only the berry that's not poisonous."

"And you know this how?" Mark asked.

"Everyone does," Charley said. "It's a yew bush. They're all over the place." She pointed out the window. "See, there. And there. And there."

"Are you telling me that Kingston is full of poisonous plants? What is wrong with you people?"

"It's not only here. They're all over the province."

"I've never heard of them before."

"I don't know. Maybe yew bushes are especially popular with gardeners in Kingston? They are mostly ornamental. But every few years you hear about a pet or a cow that has died from eating some part of the plant."

"They are poisonous enough to kill a cow?" Mark took his eyes off the road to glare at her.

She pointed out the window to direct his focus back to the task of driving. "It depends on how much of the plant you eat, I guess."

"And they're everywhere? Growing in people's gardens, waiting to be picked and used for poison?" Mark sounded incredulous. "Why are we here? Why aren't we going to the police with this?"

He eased to a stop in the laneway. Charley didn't take the time to explain. She thrust open the car door and ran up the steps to her home.

She raced past the drawing room and into the kitchen. Rachel, up to her elbows in dishwater, gaped at Charley in surprise.

"The pastries," Charley panted. "Where are they?"

"In the drawing room. I just served—"

Charley almost collided with Mark as she ran back down the hallway and into the drawing room, scanning the room for the pastries.

There! On the sideboard.

"Charlotte!" Gran reprimanded her as Charley began pulling apart the pastries looking for the poisonous seeds and their pods. "What on earth are you doing?"

No berries. No seeds. Thank goodness.

She whirled around to face eight pairs of astonished eyes staring at her. "Has anyone eaten any of these pastries?"

Bessie frowned. "No. We were playing one more hand while the tea steeped."

Charley collapsed into her chair and breathed a sigh of relief.

Mark strode into the room. "I spoke with Rachel and she hasn't eaten any of the pastries."

"Well, of course, she hasn't!" Bessie cast him an annoyed glance and then emitted a small gasp as she saw his bruised face. She didn't comment on it, though. Instead, she pushed back her chair and stood up. Placing her hands on her hips, she gave them a piercing stare. "Would one of you mind telling me what on earth is going on?"

"I think the poisonings that have been happening are from yew seeds," Charley said, as if that explained everything, and then immediately regretted her indiscretion as she heard the sharp intakes of breath from the eight ladies in the room.

She leapt to her feet. "I need to call Constable Marillo."

"What did he say?" Mark asked.

"Only that he'd check into it." Charley was irritated by the Constable Marillo's quick dismissal of her theory. "He hung up on me when I suggested they re-autopsy Barbara Young to look for yew seeds."

At least Mark hadn't thought her crazy when she told him they needed to get to Claire Zammit's bakery right away.

"So, let me get this straight," he said, as he backed out of the Stormont laneway. "You think the doc either figured out what was going on or she discovered the perpetrator in the act of putting the berries into the pastries. She confronted him in the nurses' lunch room, and he attacked her."

"And then he must have taken off with the pastries to hide the evidence."

"Maybe the police confiscated the pastries at the scene?"

"Not based on Constable Marillo's reaction to my theory," Charley said.

"And the two doctors involved, you believe, are the ones we saw Superintendent Marlow disciplining when we interviewed her the other day?"

"Maloney, the one doing the deliveries, was for certain.

I recognized him this morning when he dropped off Gran's order. I am assuming the one who discovered Laine was the other one we saw, the more polite one."

"If she was attacked by a doctor, it would explain why no one thought it odd that he was bloodied wandering down the hospital corridor." Mark took a sharp right into the small parking lot for Zammit's Fine Pastry Shoppe. "Although carrying a box of pastries might have raised a few eyebrows."

"Maybe they were in it together," Charley suggested. "Maybe Wells took the pastries and disposed of them before going back and 'discovering' Laine."

Mark turned off the engine. "It's possible, but I think it's more likely he would have let someone else find her. Besides, if she recovers, she may be able to identify her assailant or assailants. If Wells was involved, he'd want to avoid that. They told us after they found her that a few more minutes and Laine would have died for sure."

If she recovers?

Of course, Laine was going to recover. She had to.

The door to the bakery was locked. A sign in the window said it was closed Fridays and wouldn't reopen until 6 a.m. Saturday.

Charley walked around the small, grey brick building. Her frustrated slap of the wall was as effective as Mark's rattling of the locked door's handle.

Now what?

"We didn't think Claire Zammit was involved anyway," Mark said when she reappeared after walking the circumference of the building.

"No, but she could have told us more about Brett Maloney."

"Hospital admin could do that, too," Mark said.

"Yeah, but hospital admin probably has strict rules about who they give information to, and you no longer have a badge, Detective."

"Are you doubting my silver-tongued charm?" Mark's lips quirked up in a half smile.

"I just wish we had our best researcher." She swallowed the threatening sob, remembering the brave face Grace had tried to put on for their benefit. Charley needed to stay strong. If she gave in now, she would be of no use to anyone, especially Laine and Grace.

"Let's go see how she's doing," Mark said, taking Charley's arm and directing her back to his sedan.

As he opened her door, a dilapidated, powder blue Studebaker pulled up beside them. Claire Zammit sat behind the wheel.

"Are you looking for me?" she asked pleasantly as she rounded her vehicle to open the passenger door and retrieve a large, wooden box with her pocketbook perched on top. She hesitated when she saw Mark's battered face, and then continued as if nothing was amiss.

First Gran and now Claire Zammit? Charley wondered what it was about Mark that no one thought it unusual for him to have a banged-up face. But then, she hadn't commented, either—hadn't even asked him how he was feeling today. He liked to present himself as a loner who didn't need anyone. He wouldn't appreciate her concern—at least that's what she told herself.

It wasn't why she hadn't done it, though. Asking about his injury would mean having to talk about what had happened last night—about his announcement that he was Dan's half-brother. It had surprised her; he had been adamant about keeping it a secret. What she didn't know—and wasn't sure she wanted to—was why he'd chosen to reveal it at that particular moment? Had he done it for her, in retaliation to Dan's hurtful actions? Or had he done it for himself, seizing the opportunity to best a rival when he was down?

"We're not open to customers on Fridays," Claire said, interrupting her thoughts. She led them to the bakery's entrance and handed the box to Mark while she withdrew her key to unlock the door. "Come on in. You can put the box over there." She pointed to the far end of the counter-top. Once Mark had done as she asked, she gave a deep sigh —of fatigue or resignation, Charley wasn't sure. "Now, what can I do for you?" she asked.

"We wanted to ask you about your delivery man," Mark said.

"Brett?" Her hand flew to her platinum hair and she seemed flustered. "He's a medical student. Always polite. A good worker. He's not in trouble, is he?" Her eyes widened as another thought occurred to her. "You're not suggesting he's tied up in what happened to those poor girls...oh my."

"We'd like to know a bit more about him," Charley said, keeping her tone even so as not to upset her. "How long has he worked for you?"

"Just a month or so. He needed a little extra money and I needed someone to do deliveries one day a week. My mother had a fall at the end of July. She is in a convalescent home that we can't afford. I go and help on Fridays. It keeps our costs down." She motioned to the box she had brought in. "I bring them a dozen loaves of fresh-baked bread, too."

"How does it work with you not being open on Fridays?" Mark asked.

"I do the baking, based on the orders I receive. For the last month, we have been closed to walk-ins on Fridays. It's an inconvenience to many of my customers, but Friday was the best day for both Brett and me."

"What time does he come to collect the orders?" Charley asked.

"Usually around eight."

"And how long do the deliveries take?" Charley was trying to form a timeline in her head. He had picked up the orders at eight and Laine had been attacked sometime before 9:45 a.m. What time had Charley seen him? It must have been closer to 10:30. Would that be normal or late for a delivery?

"It all depends on how many orders we have. Today was especially busy. I think with the heat, fewer people were wanting to bake." She chuckled. "And of course, he had his penance order on top of all the others."

"You know about that?" Mark asked.

"Oh sure. There is little that goes on in the hospitals that I don't know about. Brett ran afoul of Super, which, between you and me, isn't hard to do. I felt sorry for the boy and was tempted to give him an extra discount on the pastries, but I knew Geneva and Super would have my hide if I did, so he paid full price."

"Do you know where he is now?" Mark asked.

Claire glanced at the clock on the wall. "I expect he'll be here at any moment. He comes around this time every week to get his pay."

"Do you mind if we wait so we can speak to him?" Charley asked. She ignored the exaggerated rolling of Mark's eyes. He may not feel the need to ask permission to stay, but she was still Bessie Stormont's granddaughter and knew the value of good manners.

"Of course not. I don't have anything to drink, but I can offer you a *mille-feuille* while you wait. I keep them in the icebox—in this heat, the *crème pâtissière* would curdle and the frosting would melt into a gooey mess."

Charley declined, but of course Mark took full advantage of the offer.

"Can I ask you some questions while we wait?" Charley asked. "I'd like to do a profile of you and your pastry shop for the *Trib*."

Mark raised his eyebrows questioningly. She shook her head. She had no ulterior motive. If they had time to kill, she would rather spend it working—a successful businesswoman was precisely the type of story she liked to promote.

"Oh, well!" Claire's cheeks flushed pink. "Do you think anyone would be interested?"

"I'm sure they'd be fascinated."

"I started baking pastries more out of necessity than anything else. I met and married my husband at the start of the Great War. I was barely eighteen." She closed her eyes and smiled at the memory. "He was so dashing in his uniform."

"Did he make it home?" Charley's voice was tight wondering whether she was going to regret asking Claire about her life.

"Oh, yes. He made it home, he survived the Spanish Flu, and we had a beautiful daughter, Maryanne."

Phew! Okay, so Claire's story wasn't the same at all.

"You would think a man would be happy with that, wouldn't you? We had a loving marriage. A perfect daughter. He had a good job working in the shipyard." She turned to Mark. "What more could a man want?"

Mark shifted uncomfortably. "I've long given up trying to figure out the wants of men."

Claire nodded. "Me, too." She returned her focus to Charley. "One morning, same as every other morning, he ate his breakfast, kissed me and the baby goodbye, and left for work. Only he never got there. He started driving and kept going." She shrugged.

"Do you know where he went? Did you ever hear from him again?"

"No, not a peep." She paused, took a deep breath and continued. "So, there I was with a wee baby and no husband to support us. My parents did what they could to help, and Geneva, too. But I was too proud to keep taking from them. I had always been a clever baker, so I started making fancy birthday cakes for the children of our friends. It grew from there."

"What about your daughter?"

"Maryanne is married with her own wee ones." She beamed. "She lives around the corner from me now."

"And you never remarried?" Mark asked.

Claire gaped at him but directed her response to Charley. "How could I? I am still married in the eyes of the Lord."

How could she, indeed. Charley understood Claire's reluctance to start again with someone new, but it wasn't the same. Theo hadn't chosen to leave her—at least Charley didn't think so.

"Anyway, after the war and rationing ended, business picked up and I decided to make the leap to a full bakery and took out a lease on this building. Before then, it had been only the fancies that I made. I hired two war veterans who work overnight to make the breads for the next day. They prefer to work when no one else is here. They enjoy the quiet, they say." She turned to Mark. "War must be a loud business. Every soldier I know has said the best part of returning home was the quiet."

Mark grunted and licked the icing from his fingers.

"Would you like another, Detective?" Claire asked.

"If it's not too much trouble." He held out his plate.

Claire went to the icebox. "I had been planning to hire a girl to help out during the daytime so I wouldn't have to close midday while I deliver the fancies," she said, her voice easily carrying from across the counter. She returned the plate to Mark with two pastries this time. "But with Mum's fall, I can't afford it right now."

The bell above the front door jingled as the door opened and Brett Maloney meandered into the shop whistling *I'm Looking Over a Four Leaf Clover*, a catchy tune Charley remembered dancing to at a fundraiser Dan had tricked her into going to with him.

"Oh, hey, sorry Mrs. Zee. I didn't know you had company. Do you want me to come back later?" he asked.

"No, Brett, these folks are here to speak with you," Claire said.

He stepped farther into the room, his eyes following Mark who was casually making his way to block the front door. Brett must have sensed he was in danger as his eyes widened in alarm. In an instant, he turned on his heel, wrenched open the door and darted out of the building.

Mark was out the door after him. Charley followed but paused on the threshold as she saw a police cruiser screech to a halt in front of the pastry shop and Constable Adams leap out to join in the chase.

"Oh, dear, Brett, what have you gotten yourself into?" Claire muttered from behind her.

Charley glared at Constable Marillo as he entered the bakery and removed his cap. "How nice of you to join us, Constable."

"Always a pleasure, Mrs. Hall." He smiled amicably, deliberately ignoring her sarcasm. He turned to Claire.

"And you are Mrs. Zammit, owner of the bakery, I presume?"

Before she had a chance to reply, the bells above the door jingled again as Mark and Adams thrust their captive into the room.

"Brett Maloney," Marillo said facing them, "you're under arrest for the attempted murder of Laine Black. And that's just for starters."

CHARLEY TOOK a sip of coffee and leaned back in the reclining chair someone had generously moved into Laine's hospital room. It was a marked improvement from the solid, upright chairs the hospital usually provided and a credit to Laine's popularity among the staff. Charley and Grace had been spelling each other off for the weekend. Grace didn't want Laine to be alone, and although the hospital staff would be more than willing to sit with her, she would only agree to leave once Charley arrived to take over. They would have to rely on the staff tomorrow when she and Grace were expected to return to work.

It would have been less wearying if there had been three of them to sit vigil, but Freddie was lost to them for now. He had found solace in a bottle, his new-found sobriety shattered along with Laine's precious skull.

Charley took another sip of the horrible hospital coffee and stared at her friend. Her petite form was barely visible, consumed by the enormous metal chamber. Only the rhythmic whoosh of air from the contraption provided any reassurance she was breathing and thus, still alive.

The heat wave that had blanketed the city for the past week persisted. The emergency room was a hub of activity as more and more heatstroke victims arrived. It was the poor and the elderly everyone was most concerned about. Already there had been several deaths. Thank heavens Rachel was keeping a close eye on Gran, making sure she drank plenty of water and took regular cooling baths.

She stood and paced the room. A copy of yesterday's *Tribune* lay on the floor. She picked it up. She had read it cover-to-cover several times—she should have tossed it in the trash after the first time—but she took it back to the chair again, anyway. The cover story was Lester Pyne's piece about the arrest of Dr. Brett Maloney. Under normal circumstances, she would resent him being given what should have been her story, but she'd been happy to let him have it. It hit too close to home. As usual, Pyne's article contained just the facts he had been given by the police and none of the richness Charley would have added.

Maloney's arrest was the talk of the hospital, too. Some —mostly the male doctors—expressed disbelief and proclaimed his innocence, while others—mostly the nurses and female doctors—were less compassionate and felt tremendous relief.

She continued flipping through the pages, knowing what was coming and wondering why she was going to deliberately torture herself with it again.

It was a lovely photograph. Dan looked fashionably handsome in a double-breasted pinstripe suit and matching vest, with a white shirt and wide, unadorned tie, secured with the gold Queen's University Rowing Team tie clip he loved. His hair was slicked back. She'd never seen him wear it that way before. Was that the fashion of an up-and-coming federal politician?

While Dan looked directly at the camera, Meredith, his *fiancée*, stared up at him doe-eyed. She wore a modest evening gown and bolero jacket with capped sleeves.

THE ALDERMAN TAKES A WIFE

Charley winced at the headline Mildred Preston had written.

"Hey," a voice said from the doorway.

Charley quickly folded the newspaper and tucked it under her chair. Unlike his photograph, today Dan was dressed casually in a green-and-white, knit sport shirt and khaki pants. His hair was ruffled as she was accustomed to seeing it.

"How'd you find me?" She'd been avoiding his telephone calls ever since Thursday, telling herself he deserved a bit of his own medicine, but in reality, too scared to expose her still-raw pain.

"Your grandmother said you'd be here."

Great! How could Gran betray her like that?

"Don't be mad at her," he stepped farther into the room. "She gave me a piece of her mind before she told me where you were."

"In that case, I'm sure there's nothing for me to say. A tongue-lashing from Bessie Stormont should more than suffice."

"Don't be like that. We need to talk." He'd stopped directly in front of her and she had to crane her neck to look up at him. A fine beading of sweat dotted his forehead and upper lip; his face was flushed.

Charley righted the recliner and stood. He still had a good five inches on her, but she felt more in control on her feet and moving about the room. "Okay but keep your voice down." She gestured to Laine. "I don't want to upset her."

Dan glanced toward the machine and his brows furrowed with concern. "I've asked the hospital to keep me apprised of any changes in her condition. I am sorry,

Charley, for you and Grace. I know she was a great friend to you both."

"Is!" Charley corrected him. "She *is* a great friend." Her anger toward him dissipated slightly. As city alderman for the area, of course he would want to be kept informed of the condition of a victim of a vicious attack, but she knew it was more than that. He genuinely cared about people in general —and about Charley, in particular.

"Of course. Sorry," he said. "I also hear you were instrumental in finding and apprehending the perpetrator."

She wasn't surprised that he'd know that too, even though it had been kept out of the papers. She shrugged. In the end, seeing Brett Maloney arrested had provided little satisfaction given the gravity of Laine's injuries.

"Look, Charley, I'm very sorry about what happened Thursday night," Dan said.

"What exactly are you sorry about?" Despite best efforts to avoid doing so, she had been thinking about this a lot, trying to separate her anger from her hurt. "Are you sorry that I was there to see it? Are you sorry I know about it? Are you sorry that I found out from someone else? That you didn't have the decency—or is it the guts—to tell me yourself?"

Dan bowed his head. "All of it. I'm sorry for all of it."

"Do you love her?"

It seemed like a logical question to her, but Dan seemed taken aback by it. "How can I love someone I hardly know?" he asked incredulously.

"How can you marry someone you don't love?"

"I'd have expected you, more than anyone, would understand that love and marriage don't necessarily go hand-in-glove."

She winced at the direct hit. He knew all her weaknesses. He knew she hadn't been in love with Theo when she'd married him—that she'd done it because he was heading off to war, because her brother—and Theo—had asked her to.

"You're right, I do," she said softly. She turned away from him. "I also know what it costs."

"If you had given me any indication...any glimmer of hope..."

How dare you put this on me?

She whirled toward him prepared to lash out, then stopped herself. This *was* on her.

Dan had always been clear about what he wanted for them. She had been the one who wouldn't commit.

"I should have told you myself," Dan said. "I had every intention of doing so. But it all happened so fast after the convention. Banks agreed to become my campaign manager and everything steamrolled from there." He took a step forward. "Jeepers, Charley, I'm almost thirty. It's time I was married and settled down."

"Is that you talking? Or your campaign manager?"

"Both." He raked his hand through his hair, the spiky mess added to the look of desperation he gave her. "Look, Charley, if you can promise me now, at this instant, that you'll marry me, I'll call off the wedding to Meredith. I'll lose Colin's support, but I don't care."

The mechanical lung expelled a great *whoosh* into the silence that followed Dan's declaration. Charley's own lungs felt as if a great weight had forced out all their air, leaving her dizzy. She grabbed the windowsill for support.

I'll call off the wedding to Meredith.

All she had to do was agree to marry him.

Wasn't that what she wanted? She only had to say "yes."

It was up to her.

But then, hadn't it always been?

She was both physically and emotionally depleted by the inevitability. Dan's offer changed nothing. She couldn't marry him as long as Theo's fate remained unknown.

This is it, then.

The end.

Her vision blurred and she gazed at Dan through a film of tears. "I can't." Behind her back, she crossed her fingers, not because it was a lie but because she wished it was.

⚬———— ————⚬

"How's she doing?"

Charley must have dozed off because Mark's sudden appearance startled her.

He held out a thermos mug. "Coffee?"

She took it and sniffed it suspiciously. She'd had just about all the hospital coffee her stomach could handle.

"Compliments of your grandmother," he said, "along with some sandwiches." He handed her a picnic hamper.

She took a sip of the strong, dark coffee. *Heaven.* "No pastries, I hope." She peered inside relieved to see a pair of brown paper-wrapped sandwiches and a couple of apples.

Mark was standing at Laine's bedside, gazing down at her immobile form.

"The doctor was by earlier. There's no change," she told him.

He pulled a wooden chair over to Charley and sat down. He accepted the sandwich she offered but didn't immediately unwrap it. "You don't look so good," he said, leaning in to examine her face more closely.

She lowered her head to hide her reaction to the truth of

his statement. She was *not so good*. In the few hours since Dan's visit, she had done little except replay their conversation and question whether she'd made the right decision or had ruined her life for all time. Mark was unlikely to be sympathetic, so she brushed off his concern. "Gee, thanks. That's what a woman likes to hear. You sure have a way with the ladies, Detective."

He frowned, not buying her bravado, but fortunately, he didn't press her on it.

"So, were you visiting my grandmother or just hitting her up for food?" Charley asked, to change the subject.

"I was looking for you. The food was a happy consequence." He still hadn't unwrapped his sandwich and the vein at his temple was pulsing. It tended to do that when he was upset.

"What's wrong?"

"I was at the police station a little while ago. They're releasing Brett Maloney."

"On bail?" She thought his hearing was tomorrow.

"No. They're completely dropping all the charges."

Charley had lost her appetite. She re-wrapped the half-eaten sandwich and dropped it back into the hamper. "How can they do that?"

"Apparently, he has an alibi for the time Doc, here, was attacked." Mark reached into his pocket and withdrew his notebook. "I had Marillo give me the details. He wasn't too happy about it—thinks he was forced to act too quickly and ended up being sloppy in his investigation."

"Let me guess, he blames me for that."

"Us, actually. But he's a big boy. He'll survive." Mark flipped through the pages. "Okay, according to Claire Zammit, Maloney picked up the pastries at 8:10. His first stop was the hospital, at 8:30, because he had a large number of deliveries to make and was afraid if he got held up, he'd miss the nurses' break time, risking the wrath of Superintendent Marlow. From 8:30 on, the cops checked with all the people to whom deliveries were made and that boy was hopping, up to and including when you saw him around 10:30—well after Laine was attacked." He closed the book and shrugged. "It wasn't Maloney."

"Well, maybe not for Laine, but what about the other incidents? The nurses' reunion...the shower...Wendy Walker and Barbara Young?"

"There's not enough evidence."

"And what about the yew berry and the crumbs Laine was holding? Are the police, at least, willing to consider that the other incidents were poisonings and open an investigation?"

"Marillo wouldn't say. I do know that it's too late to re-autopsy either Wendy Walker or Barbara Young."

"Are they going to talk to the others and see if they remember seeing berries in the pastries?"

Mark shrugged. "Even if they did, it doesn't prove who did it."

"We *know* who did it!"

"Do we?"

"Maybe he and Mitch Wells are in it together? Wells could have been the one who attacked Laine."

"Except he has an airtight alibi, too. He was doing rounds from 8:00 right up until the time he discovered Laine at 9:45. According to Marillo, a number of the hospital staff members have vouched for him."

Charley rose and paced the room, her fists balled in frustration. "So that's it?"

"I didn't say that—only that Maloney and Wells are off the suspect list, at least for the time being."

Charley paused beside Laine's bed and looked down at her friend. "Who would do this to you?" she said, gently cupping her bandaged cheek. She turned to Mark. "What's the next step? The yew?"

"Exactly," Mark said coming to stand beside her. "If we assume they were deliberate poisonings and the yew berry was the source—"

"The yew seed," Charley corrected. "The berry itself is fine."

"Sorry, I forgot. Tasty, you said, right?"

"Yeah. Kinda sweet."

"Anyway!" He sighed. "I keep wondering why, if they were all eating the same thing, wasn't everyone poisoned? Were the berries—sorry, seeds—only in some of the pastries?"

"And why would some people be more seriously affected? Was it a simple matter that Wendy Walker and Barbara Young ate more pastries than the others?"

"If we could better understand how the yew poison works, we could maybe figure out why the perpetrator chose it. What did they hope to accomplish? Did they mean for someone to die or did they intend to injure or scare?"

"I see what you're saying. If the weapon is a knife or a gun, then it's pretty obvious that a person's intention is murder," Charley said. "But wait! What about self-defence?"

"That goes to motive. The intention is still death."

"But with a poisoning it's harder to know what the perpetrator intended, right?" Charley resumed her pacing. "I am certain Laine was attacked because she'd figured out who was behind the poisoning, so in her case, the perpetrator was likely the person doing the poisoning, or someone involved in it. And I was just as sure we had a perfect

BRENDA GAYLE

motive for Maloney, and even Wells. They are hostile to women working in the hospital." She blew out her frustration. "It's as if we are back at the beginning. We have no motive for the poisonings."

"You don't always need to know the motive to figure out the crime," Mark said. "If we knew more about this particular weapon, I'm certain we'd be a lot closer to figuring out who did it."

"In that case, things may be looking up," Charley said with a spark of hopeful anticipation. "I happen to know someone who can help us."

Even by penitentiary standards, Kingston's Prison for Women was a dismal place. Almost as soon as it opened, fourteen years previously, there were calls to shut it down given its disgraceful condition. Apparently, improvements had been made, but if so, Charley could not imagine what it must have been like in 1934 when the first female inmates took up residence.

Unlike where the men were housed in Kingston Penitentiary, across the street, the women's prison didn't have guard towers. Instead, the limestone building, with its green copper roof, was surrounded by a sixteen-foot stone wall with an additional ten feet of woven wire and topped with six lines of barbed wire. Landscaping around the building was minimal. The grass, brown and dried from the heat wave that had finally broken, crackled beneath their feet as they followed one of the prison matrons from the gate into the administration building.

It had taken several days to get all the proper permissions for their visit. Charley wasn't the problem; she'd been a regular visitor over the past few months and was well known among the staff. It was Mark. Aside from the doctor and chaplain, who came from Kingston Pen, men were not common visitors to the women's prison.

"Woohoo, honey, come to Mama!"

"Hey, big boy!"

"You looking for me?"

"Hubba hubba handsome!"

Charley bit her lip to stifle a grin, glancing at Mark as they followed the matron along the walkway to the schoolroom. He was stoically keeping his eyes forward, ignoring the women's catcalls from their cells.

"Nah, he's a cop. I can smell him a mile away."

"I don't care. Cop or no, I'll take ya, honey."

Matron Burrows locked the gate as they exited the cell block and pointed to the door at the end of the corridor. "You can go and wait in there. I'll bring the prisoner to you."

Charley pulled out a wooden chair that was tucked into one of the twelve desks neatly lined up in three rows of four. "I guess you're more used to seeing criminals before they go to prison," she said, assuming Mark's stoic expression was a result of his unease. "Coming to one takes some getting used to."

Mark dragged a chair over to where she sat. "You think being here makes me uncomfortable?"

"Judging by your reaction out there? Yes."

He cocked his head. "What would you have had me do? It is hardly the first time I've been propositioned inside a prison. No point setting those girls up for something they can never have." He winked at her.

The arrogance!

"I was merely expressing concern for you. I guess I shouldn't have bothered." She angled her chair away from him. She should have insisted she come alone.

"Your concern is appreciated, but I expect I have more experience inside prisons than you have." He brought his chair around beside hers. "You know about my mother's sordid past. Did I mention I was born in Toronto's Don Jail?"

Before Charley could even think of a response, the door opened and Fiona MacDonald entered the room, followed by the matron.

"Well, hello, Missus," she said, smiling at Charley. "I was hoping it was you coming to see me. But you!" She shifted her attention to Mark and her expression darkened. "I was told there was a gentleman here, but I don't see one for looking. By the way, that's quite the shiner you're sporting. My regards to the laddie who slugged ya."

"I don't want to upset you, Miss MacDonald," Mark said, rising. "If you'd rather I leave..."

"What I'd rather, Detective..." her fierce tone matched her expression, "...is if you'd brought me some of those sweeties you used to bring the bairns." She glanced back at the woman who remained standing by the door. "But I suppose if you did, they'd have been confiscated by Matron, here, before they'd get to me." She turned back to Mark and grinned. "I'm just fussing with ya, Detective. I hold no hard feelings toward ya. I mind you were doing your job, aye?"

Looking relieved, Mark spun his chair around to the other side of the desk and indicated for Fiona to have a seat. He walked to the next desk and dragged its chair beside Charley's.

Charley closely examined her friend. Her long, red hair was tied back with a simple ribbon but it seemed flat and dull. Her once luminous skin had taken on a greyish hue and her eyes seemed to have sunk deeper into her face. The simple cotton shift she wore hung loosely from her shoulders to her ankles. Charley couldn't tell if that was due to its poor fit or if Fiona had been losing weight. Her heart ached for her friend, but she kept her thoughts to herself. Fiona would resent her pity.

"I heard about poor, wee Dr. Black," Fiona said once she had settled.

"Yes, it's awful," Charley said.

"I didn't know you knew her?" Mark said.

"Oh, aye, I've not had the pleasure of meeting the woman in person. But she has been generous in sharing her books with me, so I feel a kinship with her."

"Her medical texts," Charley explained. "I'm sorry, Fee, I didn't think to bring any with me today. I'll talk to Grace and see what I can do for next time."

"Dinna fash yourself, Charley. I appreciate what I can get, but I'm certain Grace has more to be doing than rounding up books for the likes of me." Fiona's gaze shifted to Mark. "So, given the presence of Detective Spadina, I'm thinking this isn't a social call."

"We're stumped on a case and hoping you can help," Charley said. She gave Fiona a summary of the poisonings and what they had learned so far as well as the questions they still had.

"Well, I could have told ya it wasna Dr. Maloney if you'd have asked me beforehand," Fiona said with a note of derision.

"Why? It makes perfect sense that it would be him," Charley insisted. Despite having an alibi, she still wasn't convinced Maloney wasn't responsible in some way.

"He has no motive."

"You don't think hating women is a motive?"

"I dinna think he hates all women," Fiona said, raising her eyebrows at Charley's outburst. "Only the ones he has to work with. But to answer your question, no, I dinna think he has a motive. Think about it. It is a man's world, Charley. He is already on top. Those nurses, and even the few female medical students, they're nae threat to him. So, what if he gets his knuckles rapped a time or two by the Superintendent of Nursing? In a year he'll have graduated. Full doctor. And then the Superintendent will have to answer to him."

Fiona's words rang true. Charley had experienced the inequity herself at the *Trib* when she was ousted from her job as city reporter to make room for someone less talented, but male—his only "qualification," as far as she could tell. "I hadn't looked at it from that angle before."

"Putting motive aside, what about the method?" Mark said. "Do you know anything about this yew plant and why only some of the women seemed to be affected by its poison."

"Oh, yes, I ken the yew verra well. The tree of death we called it back home. Of course, our yew trees are different from the bushes you've got here, but likely just as deadly. They're found in the graveyard of almost every kirk—church, you ken? According to ancient lore, their roots wrapped around the bodies of the dead, feeding off them and growing strong so their boughs could be used to make bows for the King's archers."

"Lovely." Charley recoiled at the image Fiona had conjured.

"You seem to know quite a lot about them," Mark said. "Charley says she's eaten the berries from them and lived to tell the tale."

"It's not the berries that are the problem. It's just every other part of it that'll kill ya," Fiona said.

"But not everyone," Charley said. "Why would only some of the girls get sick and only a couple die from it?"

Fiona tugged at her earlobe, lost in thought. "Was it just

the berry you discovered? Do you ken whether there was the seed in it as well?"

"Oh yes, the seed was still there. I'm assuming that was what killed them."

"Aye, but only if they bit down on it. Birds eat the berries all the time, but the seeds pass right through them. It's how the plants are propagated."

"What you're saying is that if they didn't chew the seed, they wouldn't have become ill?" Mark asked.

"Precisely. And as for the lassies who died, I am assuming they helped themselves to a few more of the pastries than the others."

"Or they more thoroughly chewed their food," Mark said.

"That means the victim was left up to chance," Charley said.

"Aye, and it is possible the original intention wasn't to cause death at all," Fiona said.

"But when someone died the first time, the killer got a taste for it and he continued," Charley said.

"And will likely continue until forced to stop," Fiona added.

"This tells us a couple of things about our perpetrator," Mark said. "First, we need to concentrate our efforts on the nurses' reunion as this was the first poisoning."

"That you know of," Fiona interjected.

Mark nodded. "That we know of, you're right. But for now, let's assume it is, and he has some connection to these women—although not necessarily any particular one." Mark waited until both Fiona and Charley nodded their agreement. "Okay, second, he is somewhat passive. The fact that he uses an unreliable poison, essentially leaving the victims and the severity of their symptoms to chance, tells us he doesn't need to control the situation."

"Perhaps he sees himself as an avenging angel?" Charley suggested. "He provides the weapon but believes it is up to God's will to determine who lives or dies."

"Excellent." Mark nodded in agreement. "Third, he's not a narcissist. He doesn't need people to know he's responsible nor does he need to view his handiwork first-hand."

"Unless he's a doctor and sees it when his victims arrive at the hospital's emergency," Charley said, still reluctant to give up on her pet theory.

"It's not a doctor," Fiona said definitively. "But it *is* someone who knows the medical system. The poisonings all took place at different locations. How did they get in and out unnoticed? How did they know when and where the pastries were going to be?"

The matron cleared her throat, startling Charley. She had forgotten the woman was still in the room with them.

Fiona rose reluctantly. "I wish ya good luck. Come visit me again. You, too, Detective. Maybe try sneaking in some of those sweeties if ya can next time, aye?"

Matron Burrows held open the door for Fiona to precede her from the room. "Wait here. I'll come back to escort you out," she said.

Charley remained in her seat. She wanted to hug her friend goodbye but knew from experience it wasn't allowed. It was always hard to watch Fiona leave, knowing she was returning to a wretched prison cell where she was to spend the next thirty years in penance for murdering Mark's mother.

"There is one more thing." Fiona glanced over her

shoulder. "You keep referring to the person who did this as 'he.' But poison's a woman's tool."

Marillo glanced at his watch and stood. "All right, I'm going to call it a day."

"Can we give it a little more time?" Charley asked.

"Nah, the Constable is right. It's a bust." Mark stood and stretched.

Charley blew out her breath in frustration.

It will likely continue until stopped, Fiona had said. Apparently, she was wrong.

It had seemed the perfect next step. In the two days since they'd visited Fiona, she and Mark had managed to convince Claire Zammit to provide a variety of bakery items and persuaded Brett Maloney to deliver them to one of KGH's lunch rooms. Neither had been particularly receptive to the idea given how the negative news coverage from the weekend before had impacted their lives. Although Maloney's release had been published in both of the city's broadsheets, it had appeared as a much smaller item hidden deep on the inside pages.

Marillo hadn't been all that enthusiastic about their plan, either. However, once he was assigned to the job, he had made the best of it, playing rummy with Mark all day. They'd asked Charley if she wanted to join them, but she was afraid it would distract her from noticing someone sneaking into the room across the hall where they'd planted the pastries.

She followed Mark and Marillo to the platter of pastries.

"Waste not, want not," Mark said, popping one into his mouth.

"I'll take a few home to the Missus." Marillo returned a few to the pastry box and lowered its lid. "I am sorry, Mrs. Hall. I know how important finding the culprit is to you."

Charley thanked him and he left.

"Arrrggghhh!" She gave way to her frustration.

Mark held out the platter as compensation. She shook her head. The last thing she wanted right now was one of those darn pastries.

"It was a long shot, anyway," he said.

"It was our only shot."

"That's not true. We need to go back to the beginning and examine everything again."

"Okay, but can we do it in Laine's room? I told Grace I'd stop by to give her a break."

"You want to do it now?"

"Of course. Do you have something else planned this evening, Detective?"

Mark put down the pastry he was holding. "In that case, why don't I slip out to Joe's and pick us up a couple of sandwiches and coffee? We'll need more than a few sweets if we're going to crack this case."

Even late on a Friday afternoon, the hospital was a hive of activity. Charley had spent enough time here lately that she was able to greet by name many of the nurses and orderlies she passed in the corridor as she made her way to the elevator. Laine's room was in a special section on the second floor, reserved for the most serious cases. The nurses' station was right outside her door. Charley nodded to Donna Rusk, the duty nurse. She would be leaving shortly to go home to her husband and kids, and another nurse would start the night shift. Laine was never left alone.

"Hi there." Grace looked up from her book as Charley entered the room. "Oh dear, from the look on your face, I am guessing your trap failed."

"Spectacularly!" Charley checked on Laine.

"No change," Grace said, coming to stand beside her. She slipped her arm around Charley's waist and laid her head against her shoulder. "She will come back to us. I know she will."

"I do, too."

"It's Freddie you're most worried about, isn't it?" Grace asked.

"I'm worried about all of us, but he's the one I'm less sure is going to be okay."

"I tried calling him yesterday to see if he wanted to go sailing. He didn't." Grace heaved a sigh. "It was nine o'clock in the morning and I think he was already drunk."

"More likely still drunk," Charley said. "Thank you for trying."

"I was doing it for me as much as for him. I thought a few hours on the lake would help me cope better with all this."

"Is there anything I can do for you?" Charley asked.

"Catch the bastard who did this to her," Grace said with uncharacteristic ferocity.

"That's the plan. Detective Spadina is meeting me here shortly." Charley wrapped her arms around Grace and pulled her close. She closed her eyes and prayed she and Mark would be successful, not just for Laine and Wendy and Barbara, but for Freddie and Grace, and all of them.

"I've got something for you." Grace stepped away and retrieved a manila-coloured envelope with the *Tribune*'s logo on it. "You didn't ask—which surprises me a bit." She gave Charley a piercing stare. "But I figured you'd want this anyway."

Charley opened the envelope and took out a single page. Typed in bold letters across the top: BANKS FAMILY RESEARCH. She looked up from the paper. "You're right. I didn't ask."

Grace shrugged. "I didn't know if it was because you didn't want to impose, or if you weren't interested. I know you, Charley, so I assumed it was the first."

She had considered asking Grace to investigate Colin and Meredith Banks. At first it had seemed vital to know who these people were. But that was before she had definitively refused Dan's proposal, effectively ending any right she had to influence his decisions. Did it matter now where the pair had come from and how they'd gotten their clutches—

Stop it, Charley!

—how they'd become so important to him in such a short time?

Curiosity got the better of her, if only because yesterday she'd received a strange invitation to tea from Adeline Banks. She would have loved to ignore it or, better yet, sent it back to the woman with a stark "REFUSED" scrawled across it. But Gran had taught her better than that. If Adeline wanted to make amends, she should at least give her the opportunity—if not for herself, then for Dan who was joining her family.

She scanned the page. "There's almost nothing here."

"I know. It's very strange, but I couldn't find anything about the Banks family before they bought their house on

Front Road in the spring of '46. It's like they appeared out of thin air."

"That's hardly likely," Charley frowned. "Colin Banks has an accent. Perhaps they immigrated after the war."

"That would make sense, I guess." Grace chewed her lip.

"But?"

"Whether they came from another province or another country, I should be able to find *something*."

"You found out when they arrived in Kingston—"

"When they bought their house here," Grace interjected.

"You found out Colin Banks owns a lot of properties in the downtown business district." Charley scanned the list of addresses. Mostly retail. "Hmmm. Turns out he's Detective Spadina's landlord."

Curiosity would take Charley so far. She was not going to ask Mark to probe Dan's future brother-in-law.

"I can keep digging," Grace offered.

"No, don't bother." She slid the page back into the envelop and handed it to Grace. "I appreciate you thinking of me, but I have no use for this information now."

"I DIDN'T MEAN to take so long," Mark said, balancing two take-away boxes as he entered the room. "I made a couple of telephone calls, but I'll tell you about that after we've eaten."

Charley put down the notebook she had been writing in and accepted one of the containers. "I've been trying to list what was different today compared with the last few Fridays." She lifted the lid. "Meatloaf?"

Mark nodded. "And peas and mashed potatoes. Gillian didn't think sandwiches for dinner would cut it."

"What? No pie?"

"I figured we'd had enough sweets with all those pastries, earlier."

"One of us did, at least." She carved off a corner of the loaf with her fork and took a bite. *Heaven.* "I don't think I've had meatloaf since rationing ended. It's delicious."

"You should consort with us common folk more often, Tiger. We eat all sorts of delicious foods."

She kept her head bowed and focused on the meal. Mark probably meant his comment as a joke, but she felt as if he'd slapped her. She didn't believe she was superior to him—or anyone—and yet he seemed to go out of his way to highlight their differences, both financial and social. Yes, she'd been fortunate, raised in a wealthy family, surrounded by people who cared for her. But that didn't mean her life was always rosy, that she hadn't had her share of heartbreak and loss. Maybe it wasn't the same as being raised in an orphanage, but Mark seemed to have done well enough for himself. She would never use his upbringing against him.

No, Charley envied him.

Mark Spadina may have been alone in the world, but he had the freedom to do as he pleased and be whomever he wanted. Meanwhile, Charlotte Stormont was subject to the rules of both her gender and her social station. Only as Charley Hall was she given any leeway to tweak them—and even then, it was within certain, well-prescribed, very narrow limits.

I guess the grass really is greener on the other side of the fence.

A nurse Charley didn't recognize entered the room and introduced herself as Sheila Goodson. She was considerably older than most of the nurses in the hospital, closer in age, probably, to Mrs. Pecker. "I have a bad back and haven't worked full-time in years," she said. "These days, I only come in on holidays, to give the girls a break."

Charley had forgotten Monday was Labour Day. The nurse walked to Laine's side and checked her vital signs.

"Is there any change?" Charley said coming to stand beside her.

"Not compared to the notes I've been given." She shook her head. "I've always been very fond of Dr. Black. I asked Super to assign me to this ward so I can keep an eye on her."

"You must have a lot of knowledge about the hospital and the people here," Mark said.

"Oh yes, even though I'm not here every day, I keep in

touch with many of my old friends. Of course, fewer and fewer still work here."

"You know Superintendent Marlow, though?"

"Do I know her?" Sheila chuckled. "I trained her. She worked in my ward when she was a student. I was head nurse and I'll tell you, I never saw anyone less likely to succeed. But she showed us. I was just commenting to Geneva—"

"Geneva Pecker?" Charley asked.

"Yes. She and I are old friends. I worked for her father for a time. That was right after I graduated. Her mother was a frail thing and would have long periods of time when she couldn't work. Once she recovered, I came here."

"Tell us more about Superintendent Marlow," Mark said.

"I don't like to gossip," she said, obviously regretting her earlier disclosure. "All I will say, however—and I'm sure she'd agree—is that she is a better administrator than a nurse." Sheila gave Laine a final look and headed to the door. "I'll be just outside if you need me."

"Why are you so curious about Superintendent Marlow?" Charley asked Mark. "I've been going over everything that was different today and I keep coming back to Geneva Pecker."

"How so?"

"We went directly to Claire Zammit with our order, bypassing the route all the hospital workers would have had to take."

"We don't know if Brett Maloney went through Mrs. Pecker. He could have ordered directly from Claire."

"That's true. But even if she didn't place the order, she knew about it." Charley flipped through her notebook. "Claire told us she made him pay the regular price for the pastries because Geneva and Super would, quote, 'have her hide' if they found out she'd given him an extra discount." Charley could see Mark still wasn't convinced. "And don't forget, at the nurses' reunion, no one at Mrs. Pecker's table fell ill."

"It could be a coincidence. Fiona told us how the poison works."

"Sure, a whole table of seed-swallowers," Charley said with disdain. "Or maybe none of their pastries had the berries in them."

"How old would you say Geneva Pecker is?"

"Mid-fifties."

She knew where Mark was going with this. "Laine is tiny, five feet on a good day. It's not inconceivable that her attacker was a woman."

"I agree. But Laine is young, and she is fit. I don't think Geneva Pecker has the strength or disposition to do it."

"But Superintendent Marlow does?"

"Yes, I believe so."

"Okay, Detective, convince me."

"Beginning with the reunion. Three of the four victims were at her table. One of them, the one with whom she just so happened to have an antagonistic relationship, died."

"Yes, but she explained that. She asked Wendy to sit at her table so she could subtly offer her support."

"Says she. But I made a few calls earlier this evening and none of the other nurses at the table remember them having that conversation. In fact, every one of them commented that it felt awkward at the table because the two were so often at odds and didn't have much to say to one another at the tea."

"So, she lied."

"Don't sound so disappointed, Tiger. Most criminals do."

Charley was disappointed. She had been so impressed by Marlow's intention to work with Wendy behind the scenes to help improve conditions for the nurses. Learning the truth felt like a betrayal, not just to the nurses she was supposed to represent but to all women who were trying to gain the respect of men in the workplace. "You must have more."

"As Superintendent of Nursing, Marlow can easily travel between the two hospitals. No one would think it odd to find her at Hotel Dieu as she often coordinates with the superintendent of nursing there."

"But what about the attack on Laine? It would be odd to see the superintendent of nursing covered in blood. She doesn't tend to patients."

"The most any witness is likely to observe is a nurse, dressed in white like every other nurse, running down the hallway, presumably responding to an emergency. Patients and visitors don't know who she is. And hospital staff aren't likely to find anything odd about the behaviour, so they wouldn't give her a second look."

Charley tapped her pen against her notebook. It was all circumstantial, but Mark was making some sense.

"Do you want to hear more?" he asked.

"Do you have more?"

"When we interviewed her, she told us how scared all the women who work in the hospital were. And yet, when she meted out her punishment to Brett Maloney, she had him buy pastries for the nurses."

"Because he worked at the bakery."

"So what? He wasn't getting them for free. She could have had him buy cold colas for everyone. We were in the middle of a heat wave. Or what about sandwiches? Anything else but pastries."

"It would be easier to hide the berries in pastries."

"Yes, she'd been successful with them before. Plus, she had him do it on a Friday."

"That's when he made his deliveries for Mrs. Zammit."

"That doesn't mean he couldn't have picked them up any other day of the week. Again, why did it have to be pastries? And why did it have to be Friday?"

"Pattern? Routine?"

"Ask yourself this: why do it at all? Laine told you that the nurses and female docs had already decided not to have any more special gatherings. They were scared. Superintendent Marlow prided herself on having her ear to the ground, so to speak. She had to have known that. And yet, she sets up a situation that is guaranteed to bring them together. I mean, Zammit's Fine Pastries are delicious. Who wouldn't want to come to the ten o'clock break?"

"It was a coffee break. They probably didn't think of it as a special gathering—just a few treats, compliments of Dr. Maloney."

"Exactly. I've had my share of whoopings and punishments over the years and buying pastries doesn't begin to make the grade. If Superintendent Marlow wanted to teach Maloney and Wells a lesson, why wouldn't she have them do something more degrading? Something they would consider too menial, too embarrassing for a doctor to do?"

"It could have been what Fiona said: that in a few years they'd be full doctors and then Marlow will have to answer to them." But Mark's theory did fit a lot of the pieces together nicely. "You are starting to convince me. But what is her motive?"

Mark shrugged. "She's the only one who can tell us that."

"What are we going to do about it? Confront her?" She glanced at her watch. It was late and Marlow had probably already gone home. That didn't matter. They could easily find out where she lived. Charley was anxious to resolve this whole mess tonight, if possible. She stared at her friend, fighting for her life—if only to give them all some peace of mind.

"I think we should take what we know to Constable Marillo."

Charley couldn't have been more surprised by his response. When they had worked together in the past, Mark had shown nothing but antipathy for the Kingston police department, deeming them too small and backward compared with his former colleagues in Toronto. She wasn't sure what had happened to make him change his tune now. Maybe he and Marillo had bonded over their multiple hands of rummy earlier. "Do you think he'll listen to us?"

"He was here today, wasn't he?"

"Only because I bribed his sergeant with cinnamon cakes."

"I think we have a few pastries left."

CHARLEY THANKED Romeo Arcadi as he helped her out of his cab at the Bankses' Front Road home. She'd been surprised he answered her call, given it was Labour Day, an occasion to celebrate workers with parades and picnics organized by the trade unions. She was not surprised that he wouldn't accept her money. He never did anymore. She wondered what his employer thought of that, but that was his business. She was reluctant to appear too interested in his life for fear he'd see it as a sign she was warming to the idea of meeting his unmarried son.

She stared up at the limestone mansion. She did not want to be here. She had spent most of the weekend hoping Adeline would remember that today was a civic holiday and it was expected, in most households at least, that domestic staff be given the day off.

Adeline's invitation was one more thing for her to fret about.

Constable Marillo and Sergeant Kearn hadn't been as convinced by Mark's logic as they'd hoped. But the police officers did agree it warranted a conversation with Superintendent Marlow. Marillo's irritation at being called back to the police station late on a Friday night was compounded when they learned that Marlow had left town for the holiday weekend and was not expected to return until Tuesday morning. Charley couldn't understand why they didn't go question her at her sister's home in Bobcaygeon, but the three men all cited rules about police jurisdiction and a lack of perceived threat.

Tomorrow," she'd told Laine when she'd visited the hospital earlier in the day. "One more day and then you'll have justice."

If there was any bright spot in what had been an overall dismal weekend, it was that Laine seemed to be showing some response when spoken to. She was still unconscious, but Charley swore she could see movement beneath her closed eyelids whenever she was spoken to. The doctors urged her and Grace to temper their expectations, but what else would they say? Nurse Sheila Goodson had been less reticent, agreeing there was some cause for optimism. Charley would take whatever good news she could.

Adeline answered the door herself and ushered Charley down a hallway to the back of the house. "I set up in the breakfast nook. It's off the kitchen and, of course, the staff have the day off, so it'll be just the two of us."

"Your husband and sister-in-law aren't here?" Charley asked.

"They're at the parade."

"It's unfortunate you couldn't join them. We certainly could have arranged a different time."

"I didn't want to wait any longer," Adeline said. "I'm afraid we got off on the wrong foot and I wanted to fix that. I also wanted to thank you for the lovely article you published about Meredith's engagement."

"Well, you were right. It was big news."

"Have a seat in there. I'll go add the water to the pot and bring it to the table."

The breakfast nook was surrounded on three sides by glass windows that overlooked a flower garden with festive chrysanthemums in a riot of reds and oranges and yellows, and pretty pansies in almost every colour imaginable. A brick walkway led to a small, round table under an awning and Charley wondered why they weren't sitting outside to take advantage of the last vestiges of summer. She turned away from the window and back to her hostess who was carrying a tray from the kitchen. She remembered why. Given the amount of face makeup she applied to cover her freckles and the long-sleeved blouse she was wearing, Adeline must abhor the sun. A reluctant redhead, Charley concluded. Now, the unnatural blonde hair colour made sense.

"This is a lovely room," Charley said, choosing a chair that allowed her at least to look out at the garden.

"Yes, it is." She put the tray in the centre of the table and sat down across from Charley. "I had the cook make some cookies yesterday." She held out a tray of sugar cookies. "While you wait for the tea to steep."

Although she wasn't hungry, Charley took one to be polite and set it on the plate in front of her.

"Only one teacup?" Charley asked.

"I don't like tea, I'm afraid."

"You needn't have gone to the trouble for me," Charley said. "I would be perfectly happy with whatever you're having."

"Oh no, no, no. I invited you for *tea*. That is what is done, isn't it?" Adeline's face flushed.

Against her will, Charley found herself warming to the young woman. This was all new to her; she was trying to find her footing in a world she was not born to. "Yes, tea is what's done." Charley took a bite of the sugar cookie because actually eating the food your hostess offers you is also what's done in polite society.

"I am so terribly sorry, Mrs. Hall, about what happened at Meredith's engagement announcement," Adeline said. "I had no idea you were Daniel's friend and that he hadn't told you about Meredith."

"How could you have known? Please, Mrs. Banks, don't think about it any further. It's all water under the bridge now anyway." Charley gave herself an imaginary pat on the back for being so magnanimous.

"Adeline. You must call me Adeline." She picked up the silver teapot and poured the pale brown liquid into an elegant floral cup. "I hope it's all right," she said handing the cup and saucer to Charley. "I had cook show me how to make it yesterday." She pointed to the tray. "Lemon? Or would you prefer milk?"

"Neither, thank you. I drink it clear. And I'm sure it will be lovely." Charley glanced down at the cup. It was much paler than she liked—but then she was a coffee drinker at heart.

"Addie! Addie, where are you?" A woman's voice rang out from the front of the house. "I couldn't bear the thought of you being alone all day so I—" Meredith, dressed in forest-green capris and a matching cap-sleeve top, stopped in the doorway, her pale eyes widening in surprise. "Oh, Charl—Mrs. Hall...Charley...Can I call you Charley? Dan has told me so much about you, I feel like I know you already." She rushed toward the table. "Tea? Lovely. Let me get myself a cup."

"No, let me." Adeline pushed back her chair and jumped to her feet. She must have lost her balance because she fell against the table, sending both the tray with the teapot and Charley's cup crashing to the floor.

Charley leapt up but could not avoid the scalding liquid that fell onto her thighs.

"Oh no! How can I be so clumsy?" Adeline's eyes filled with tears. "Are you all right, Mrs. Hall?" She turned to Meredith. "And your family's lovely tea service..."

"It's all right, Addie. It was an accident." Meredith's voice was soothing. "And you, Mrs. Hall? Were you burned?"

"It's Charley, and I'm fine," she snapped, unreasonably annoyed. Immediately, she regretted her outburst. Both Adeline and Meredith appeared crushed. Poor, floundering Adeline had only wanted to make amends and sweet, considerate Meredith had returned home so her sister-in-law wouldn't be alone. Both were better women than she. Charley sighed heavily. "Thank you for your concern. I think it would be best if I left."

"Oh, no, you mustn't," Meredith said. "I feel just awful. If I hadn't interrupted you, none of this would have happened."

"Yes, please stay," Adeline said. "I can make more tea."

"All right, but don't make fresh tea on my account." The stinging of Charley's thighs had become tolerable, but her coral-coloured wrap skirt was ruined. "Can I help you clean up?"

"Oh no, please leave it. Let's go sit somewhere else." Adeline sounded relieved. She ushered them back along the hallway and into the library Charley remembered so well.

Great. This day is getting better and better.

Charley chose an armchair while Adeline and Meredith sat at opposite ends of the couch across from her. There was an uncomfortable silence and Charley dearly wished she had insisted on leaving. What on earth did she have to say to these women? Even Gran's tutelage in how to make small

BRENDA GAYLE

talk was failing her. They had nothing in common—well, except for Dan, and she was not prepared to have him be their topic of conversation.

You're a reporter. Pretend it's an assignment.

"I haven't heard of the Banks family before. Did you move to Kingston recently?" she asked Meredith.

"Colin and Meredith arrived a few years ago," Adeline answered instead. "I met Colin at a fundraiser for the hospital."

"Oh yes, I'm ever so impressed with how clever Addie is," Meredith said. "She graduated from nursing school, you know. If she hadn't married my brother, she'd be a working woman now."

Charley noted how Adeline had deftly deflected the conversation away from Colin and Meredith and any follow-up questions she might pose about where they had come from. But was that because they had something to hide? Or did she want to be the centre of attention? Charley decided to humour her for now. "Was it hard to give up nursing after you spent so much time preparing for it?"

"Not at all. I am much happier as a wife."

"Oh, Addie, that reminds me, you were going to lend me your old student nursing uniform for the costume par—"

"I got rid of that old thing eons ago," Adeline said abruptly.

"But remember, I tried it on a little while ago," Meredith's gentle voice insisted. "And I need to get it fitted—"

"You're mistaken. Please drop it!"

The fierceness of Adeline's rebuke sent Meredith scurrying from the room.

"Oh, darn it!" Adeline glared at Charley as if she was somehow responsible and then followed her sister-in-law, leaving behind a sense of *déjà vu*.

Charley told herself that now would be the perfect time to make her exit. Except she no longer felt she wanted to, and it had nothing to do with the good manners Gran had drilled into her. Something was going on.

She wandered back to the breakfast nook. She'd make herself useful—maybe regain a little goodwill—while she waited for Adeline to return.

It was possible that she was misreading the undercurrent of what she had witnessed between Adeline and Meredith. She didn't have a sister and wasn't familiar with how that dynamic worked. A brother was different—at least that's what she'd always assumed.

Oh, Freddie. Would it have been different if I had been a boy? Would you be able to confide in me then?

Charley stopped in the kitchen to get a dishrag and some towels. In the breakfast nook, she righted the teapot, then wiped off the tabletop and scooped the crumbs and shards of porcelain onto the tray. She knelt to mop up the spilled tea and noticed that droplets of liquid were still falling from her chair. As she wiped those away, she detected an odd odor.

She held the towel to her face. Then picked up a clean towel, sniffed it, and mopped up some of the tea and sniffed again. It was definitely the tea she was smelling. But it didn't smell like any tea she'd ever had before.

Woodsy? Oily?

She stood and sniffed again. Unpleasant, certainly, but there was an acute sweetness there, too—as if someone was trying to cover up the bitterness of it.

Yes, bitter—that's it!

She placed the cloths onto the tray and carried it, along with the teapot, back into the kitchen. She lifted the lid off the teapot to see what sort of tea Adeline had used and was surprised to see no tea ball or bag.

That's strange. Hadn't she said it needed to steep?

She glanced around the kitchen.

What did she use?

Adeline had said she wasn't a tea drinker, so it was possible she'd simply erred badly in the brewing process. Charley lifted the lid off a pot that was left on the cooktop. Or...

Her heart leapt into her throat and the temperature in the room plummeted. The lid rattled as she dropped it onto the counter.

She steadied herself, took a deep breath, and looked into the pot again. She picked up a ladle and prodded at the brown mush. No doubt about it. Tree bark. And nettles. She swallowed heavily. Bits of red, too—the tough skin of the berries that hadn't been absorbed into the mush. A mortar and pestle nearby held the desiccated remnants of whatever had been ground there. With sickening aware-ness, Charley knew it had been seeds. Yew seeds.

Breathe.

Take a minute.

Everything fell into place. She scanned the kitchen, spotting the telephone in the corner, and dialed Mark's tele-phone number.

Answer darn it! Answer!

"Hello?" His voice was hoarse as if he'd just woken up.

"Hang up the phone." The command from behind was softly spoken but came accompanied by the distinctive metallic crunch of the barrel of a rifle snapping into place.

CHARLEY CAREFULLY LOWERED the handset to the hook, hoping the slow momentum would maintain the connection. It might have worked with a more modern telephone, but this was an old-fashioned, candlestick model, and the weight of the receiver was too great. Her heart sank as she heard the telltale click of the line going dead.

"I never took you for a gun person. I thought poison was your weapon of choice," she said bravely

"I'll use whatever I need to."

Charley willed her heart to stop racing. She needed to keep her wits about her if she was going to get out of this alive.

"You can hardly shoot me in your kitchen. Do you have any idea how big a mess a rifle makes?"

Adeline cocked her head, considering. "You're right. I'm going to take you out back and do it there." She pointed the muzzle toward the breakfast nook and its doorway out to the garden Charley had admired earlier. "Get moving."

Charley took a deep breath and did as Adeline demanded.

Outside the sun was shining brightly and she could hear birds singing. It was an odd juxtaposition, given her current predicament. She glanced around and noticed, for the first time, the garden was ringed with yew bushes. Funny, she had been so enamored with the colourful flowers, she hadn't noticed before.

Would it have made a difference?

It seems she had overlooked a lot when it came to Adeline. Mark had warned her about leaving loose ends hanging.

"What are you going to tell the police when they find my body?" Charley asked, stalling.

"I'll say I heard an intruder. A woman alone? The police will understand."

"What about Meredith? She knows I was here for tea. Others do, too."

"I'll tell them that we'd had our tea and you left. I had no idea you had come back sneaking around the house. And as for Meredith?" Adeline's tone became scornful. "She'll say whatever she is told to say."

"I don't think you give her enough credit. She's stronger than you think." Charley looked up at the second-floor windows. "Where is she, anyway?"

"Locked in her room. It's on the other side of the house." Adeline cocked the gun.

"Wait!" Charley held up her hands. "Before you shoot me, can you at least tell me why you invited me here? I know you meant to kill me—poison me with the tea—but why? How did you see it all unfolding?"

Adeline lowered the muzzle of the rifle so that it was no longer aimed at Charley's chest. "I guess I can do that."

Is that pride on her face?

Charley felt a glimmer of hope. If she could keep her talking long enough, maybe she would become distracted or lower her guard and Charley could escape. Maybe Colin or one of the domestic staff would return home. She had to keep her talking.

"The engagement announcement was supposed to be my moment," Adeline said.

"But it was Meredith's party."

"It was *my* party. I was the hostess. I wanted something that would be in keeping with the illustrious Banks name. Meredith and Daniel wanted something small and intimate, but I knew I would be forgiven if I could pull off a truly spectacular evening. And I would have if it hadn't been for you ruining it all. Even Colin was furious with me afterward. He said he had no idea I'd gone against Meredith's wishes."

"I am so sorry, Adeline, I had no idea I messed things up so badly for you."

"Yes, well, now you see why I invited you to tea."

"But if I became ill or died, how would you have explained it?"

"I would have told them I did everything I could, but you must have had a heart condition no one knew about. I am a nurse. No one would have doubted me."

"You're right. That's very clever." Charley was chilled by Adeline's dispassionate explanation of her plan. "How did you settle on the yew bush for the poison? Did you always know about it?"

"Everyone knows the yew tree is poisonous." Her tone was dismissive.

"But the first time you used it—at the nurses' reunion— did you intend to kill Wendy Walker?"

"You want to know about that, too, do you?" She looked inordinately pleased with herself.

"I want to know about all of it. It was brilliant. You have the police well and truly stumped."

"They aren't very smart, are they?" The muzzle lowered a little more. "I got my invitation to the reunion, but I knew no one wanted me there."

"I would have thought you'd go if only to show the others how well you've done for yourself."

"Hmmph, they wouldn't have appreciated it. Even when I got my engagement ring, they weren't suitably impressed. They're a bunch of ninnies."

The hair on her neck prickled as Charley remembered what the nurses from the reunion had said about Adeline, how she was unable to empathize with the patients, even going so far as to blame them for their illnesses. She could well imagine how Adeline would view poisoning her former classmates as just recompense for their failure to kowtow to her new social status. "So, you decided to show them what's what," Charley said encouragingly.

"Exactly! This was much better," Adeline said. "I knew the drill. The student nurses would be up at the crack of dawn making sandwiches for the tea, and then off to their classes until it was time to come back and serve. Mrs. Zammit comes by with the pastries mid-morning, after which Mrs. P goes off to run her errands, leaving the house empty for an hour or more."

"That's when you did it. You slipped into her house— which would be easy for you since you used to live there— and embellished the pastries with your yew berries."

"I didn't think anyone was going to die. How many *eclairs* do you have to eat to get enough seeds to actually die?" Adeline giggled. "But if anyone could do it, it would be Wendy."

"You didn't like her very much."

"She didn't like me. None of them did."

"I see. You only wanted to make them sick enough that

it would ruin their reunion."

"I wish I'd been there to see them spewing their guts out."

Charley winced at the image but continued her questioning. She had to know why Adeline had taken things so much further. "What about the next week at Hotel Dieu? Did those nurses do something to offend you, too?"

"We may have trained at different hospitals, but we all knew each other." She scowled. "I heard they were having a baby shower for Annette. Of all those girls, I liked her best, but she didn't invite me."

"I didn't think any of the KGH nurses were invited."

"That's beside the point!"

"I understand." Charley smiled conspiratorially, but inside she felt nauseous. She was appalled by Adeline's pettiness, that such a small slight could be perceived as justification for murder. "How did you do it, then? Oh, wait. You wore your student nurse uniform, didn't you, you smart girl?"

Adeline preened. "I did. It's a little different from the Hotel Dieu one, but people see a white uniform and they don't look much closer than that."

"So, you figured out where they were holding the shower, you added the berries to their pastries—"

"It was a cake."

"Cake." Charley nodded agreeably. "And then you snuck—"

"I didn't sneak anywhere! You are making me sound like a thief skulking around. I walked in there liked I belonged."

"My apologies. I don't think I would have had the nerve, but of course, you most definitely did. After all, you do belong there, don't you?"

"You're darn tootin' I do." Adeline puffed out her chest. "No one died that time, though." She sounded disappointed. "I guess those Catholic girls are a little more refined in their eating."

"But you did want someone to die."

Adeline shrugged. "Not necessarily. I figured if they did, they'd be getting what was coming to them. Greedy little piggies."

"What made you decide to target the female doctors next?"

"Well, that's a prickly one." She frowned. "I didn't know it was the lady docs. I don't have a beef with them. I only heard Mrs. Zammit take an order for KGH."

"You heard her?"

Adeline looked at Charley as if she was an imbecile. "How do you think I found out? Mrs. P calls her sister at the bakery every Wednesday afternoon at exactly three o'clock to place her order. You can set your watch by Mrs. P and Mrs. Zee has a voice that will carry across a football field."

It was that easy?

"So, for a few weeks, I made sure to stop by to pick up breakfast croissants or a pie on Wednesday afternoons."

"Until Lai—Dr. Black caught you."

"As I said, I've got nothing against the lady docs. But that Dr. Black, she arrived and started asking questions. A Nosy Nellie, sticking her snout where it doesn't belong. I had to do something, didn't I?"

"Did she recognize you? Is that why you tried to kill her?"

"One nurse looks the same as any other to them," Adeline said derisively. "I didn't mean to hurt her. I was trying to get away."

A wary look had crept into Adeline's eyes, but Charley

pushed on, desperate to understand. "Why did you stop? Is it because you'd gotten so much blood on your uniform, you couldn't use it to move easily around the hospitals anymore?" Another thought occurred to her. Fiona had been right about the sex of the killer, and that murder may not have been the original intent. She'd also said the killer would likely continue until forced to stop. The very fact Adeline had invited Charley to tea with the intention of poisoning her seemed to suggest she intended to continue with her vindictive revenge. "I'm sure you could find another uniform. Are you planning—"

Adeline raised the muzzle of the rifle. "Enough talking. I don't want to answer any more of your questions. It's time to end this, once and for all."

"Addie, no!"

Charley swung toward the sound of the new voice as the rifle's blast pierced the air.

She froze.

Then, as the reverberations subsided, she came back to life and ran her hands down her body. Checking.

Am I shot?

Nothing hurt. She took a deep breath. Relief washed over her.

I'm okay. I'm okay.

A few yards away, Adeline was wringing her hands and wailing as she hovered over a green-clad form lying prone on the ground halfway between the house and where she'd been standing. Charley rushed toward her, kicked the rifle out of reach, and looked down.

Meredith was on her back, eyes open but she was staring at nothing. Her hands were splayed across her abdomen as blood oozed out between her fingers, trailing over her hips, and staining the stone walkway.

"SHE STARTLED ME," Adeline sobbed. "I turned just as..."

Charley crouched beside Meredith and applied pressure to her abdomen. "For God's sake, Adeline, you're a nurse, do something!"

Charley's firm command seemed to snap Adeline's inertia. She pushed Charley out of the way and took over. "I'll do that. You get some towels. And call Murdock's Funeral—he's the closest."

Charley returned with a handful of towels she had found in the linen closet, just off the kitchen. "Murdock will be here any minute," she said.

Because a hearse could accommodate a person lying down, and a funeral director often had some medical know-how, Murdock's Funeral Home, like most in the city, was often called upon to take the sick or injured to hospital.

Someone would need to keep the pressure on Meredith's wound, but the back of the hearse wasn't large enough for both her and Adeline. How was she going to ensure Meredith got to the hospital without Adeline escaping?

She would have to improvise as she went along.

Ross Murdock came directly into the backyard as Charley had instructed. Dressed more casually than any funeral director she'd ever seen, he was wearing an open-neck, white sport shirt and dark trousers. Tall and remark-ably fit for a sexagenarian, he easily carried the stretcher under his arm.

"You came by yourself?" she asked him.

"It's a holiday. I was the only one there." He dropped the stretcher beside Meredith. "You take her legs and we'll lift her onto the stretcher together," he said to Charley. "You keep up the pressure," he added to Adeline. "One, two, three, lift."

Once they got Meredith into the back of the hearse, along with Adeline, Charley climbed up into the passenger seat beside Murdock. He backed out of the laneway and then raced along Front Road, passing her home on King Street, to get to KGH. Charley had a few minutes to formu-late a plan. She was going to need Murdock's help if he was willing.

Two nurses ran out to greet the hearse as it arrived. An emergency doctor appeared seconds later and took over from Adeline.

It happened very quickly. As soon as Meredith disap-peared into the hospital, Adeline seized the opportunity to escape. She shoved Charley out of her way and started to flee. But Murdock had been warned and was ready. Adeline managed a few paces before he caught up with her and tackled her to the ground. She struggled beneath him, a wildcat fighting for her life.

Charley called out for assistance as she went to Murdock's aid. There was blood dripping from a jagged scrape on his cheek where Adeline had clawed at him.

And then Mark and Constable Marillo were there. Mark helped her and Murdock to their feet while Marillo handcuffed Adeline.

"It's Adeline! Adeline Banks is the poisoner," she said breathlessly.

Marillo nodded, urging his captive to her feet and steering her away.

"What are you doing here?" she asked Mark. She glanced over and was relieved to see a nurse leading Murdock into the emergency.

"We got to the Bankses' home in time to see the hearse leave. I don't mind telling you, that took a few years off my life. Marillo wanted to check the house, but I insisted we follow the hearse. Good thing I did."

"How did you know to go to the Bankses' in the first place? I didn't have a chance to tell you anything. I didn't even tell you it was me."

"Who else would call me on a holiday and then hang up without saying a peep?" He gave her his know-it-all grin. "It took me a while to track down where exactly you were, but once I did..." He shrugged. "I called Marillo and he came right away."

"That surprises me. I figured I'd lost all credibility with him."

"Kind of like the little boy who cried wolf too many times?"

"Exactly like that."

"He seems to have a soft spot for you."

Charley looked over Mark's shoulder. Two police cruisers had arrived. Adeline was being put into the back of one of them. Marillo was speaking with his partner, Constable Adams, and another officer. He looked up to see Charley watching him, said something to the two men, and then came toward her.

"Let me guess, you need me to come to the station to make a statement," she said.

"Yes, I do."

"Someone should be at the Bankses' house for when Colin gets home," she said. "Someone needs to tell him what's going on."

Marillo looked exasperated and Mark grinned at him.

"What?" Charley said, unreasonably annoyed by how buddy-buddy they seemed to have become.

"That is standard procedure, Mrs. Hall. Believe it or not, I have done this a time or two."

"I CAN'T WAIT to tell Laine we caught her," Charley said to Mark as they waited for Sergeant Kearn to finish reading over her statement before having her sign it. She'd spent over an hour explaining to Marillo and Adams what Adeline had confessed to her, as well as what had led to Meredith being shot. Mark, she'd filled in on the way over; he hadn't needed quite so much detail. Now it was Adeline's turn and according to the station's grapevine, she was singing like a bird.

"Charley!" Dan rushed into the lobby of the station and came toward her, his arms outstretched as if he meant to embrace her. She stepped back and his arms dropped to his side. His eyes widened in confusion.

"Why aren't you with Meredith?" she asked, getting straight to the point.

"I wanted to check on you," Dan said, running his hand through his already dishevelled hair.

"I think you gave up the role of Charley's protector when you got yourself engaged to someone else, didn't you, Sport?" Mark said, stepping closer to her.

"I didn't give up being her friend," Dan said through gritted teeth.

"You should go to Meredith," Charley insisted.

"Colin's there."

That made no sense to Charley. Why wasn't Colin here with his wife? Why wasn't Dan at the hospital with his *fiancée*? Everything was all mixed up.

"I guess this throws a wrench in your plans to run for federal office, eh Sport?"

Dan stared at him dumbly.

"Well," Mark continued, "your campaign manager's wife is about to be charged with multiple homicides and attempted murders. Doesn't bode well for your plans to marry into the family, does it?"

Charley closed her eyes and prayed Mark would stop. He was only asking what she herself had been wondering, but it wasn't his place.

Dan looked past Mark, his eyes imploring Charley—but for what? What did he want from her? They'd had this conversation already. She could not give him what he wanted.

"But then, you have to ask yourself, Sport, what kind of man abandons his critically injured *fiancée* when she's risked her life to save his—what'd you call Charley? Your friend? Is that the kind of man we want running our country?"

"Shut up!" Dan wheeled on him.

"Not in here!" Sergeant Kearns barked from behind the desk. "Take it outside, gentlemen."

"Charley?" Dan tried again, her name a plaintive cry.

"Nothing has changed," she whispered. No fingers crossed this time.

"Okay." He nodded, turned on his heel, and left.

"Here you go, Mrs. Hall. Sign here and you're done." Charley could have kissed Jerry Kearn for his knack of knowing just how and when to step in and break the tension.

"You're better off without him, you know," Mark said as they descended the stairs of the police station.

"Do you always have to antagonize him?"

"Hey, that's what brothers do, Tiger."

They crossed the deserted market square, heading to where Mark had parked his car on Brock Street. The sun was setting and there was a definite chill in the air.

"Have you ever asked yourself why you couldn't commit to Cannon?" Mark asked.

"I don't want to talk about it."

"I think you've always known that he was the wrong man for you."

"Did you hear what I said?" she snapped. "I don't want to talk about it."

"Maybe not, but you need to stop living in this dream world you've created for yourself. Someone needs to tell you the truth."

She stopped and turned to face him. "And that someone is you?"

"No one else seems to have the guts."

"Leave me alone." She stomped away, deciding to walk home rather than spend any more time with him.

"I can't do that." He easily caught up to her and took her arm, forcing her to stop and look at him. "If you were truly in love with Cannon, you'd have agreed to marry him a long time ago."

"You know why I can't."

"Ah, yes, your first husband, Mr. Theodore Arthur Hall.

You trot him out as an excuse, but six years on, it's become pretty lame."

Mark caught her hand, stopping the slap mere inches from his cheek.

"You know marrying Theo was a mistake. Just like you know marrying Cannon would be repeating that same mistake."

She wrenched her arm free. "I hate you!" The anger burning in her was scorching, roiling from deep within her gut, rising into her chest. She had never hated anyone before—not profoundly, not passionately, not with the white-hot fury that was consuming her. But as she said the words, she realized she truly meant them. She hated Mark Spadina.

It was mid-afternoon. Charley switched on the desk lamp to counter the dimness of her room. It was a dull, dreary day. The rain that had been threatening since last evening finally came. It was the first drenching the city had received in weeks and should have felt refreshing, clearing away the weighty, stagnant air that had continued to lurk long after the heat wave broke. But as the thunder rumbled and the lightning sizzled, she felt uneasy.

Unsettled.

The old adage about an ill wind that blows no one any good came to mind, and she chided herself for being foolish.

She had chosen to stay home rather than go into the *Tribune* today. She was too angry to be civil to anyone there. After Adeline's arrest, she had reminded John Sherman that the poisoning story was rightfully hers—that was the deal they had struck weeks ago when he'd sent her to the hospital at the time of the nurses' reunion. But the managing editor had feigned amnesia and given it to Pyne, who had done his usual hack job.

Now Charley was writing an article for the women's pages that she hoped would revive Claire Zammit's business. The bakery had been a victim of the media frenzy that had captivated the public with all the salacious details of

Adeline's crimes. It had been headline news for the past two days. Surely, it was time to move on to something new.

Charley promised Grace she would swing by the hospital after dinner to visit Laine. The doctors were now admitting cautious optimism that she was improving. It wasn't much but at least it was a small comfort.

She hadn't spoken to Dan since he'd come to the police station to find her. She had heard, on one of her visits with Laine, that Meredith was recovering well. The bullet had managed to miss all her vital organs and she was expected to be home by the end of the week. Charley sent flowers and a get-well note to her room—the woman had saved her life, after all.

Charley had no idea what Dan's plans were. Would he go ahead with the wedding? For Meredith's sake, she hoped he would. But also, for Meredith's sake, she hoped he wouldn't. She wouldn't wish a loveless marriage on anyone, least of all a wide-eyed romantic innocent.

She held no ill-will toward Dan. He had once been her dearest friend. She did not doubt that given time, their friendship would resume, although in a different, less cherished manner.

Mark, on the other hand...

No, she couldn't think about him—would not think about him.

How had he dared speak to her as he had? He knew nothing about her. Nothing about what Theo meant to her. *Nothing!*

Down in the laneway she watched with interest as Romeo Arcadi's black taxi glided to a stop. The cabbie exited his vehicle and opened one of the back doors, extending his hand to assist its occupant. On the other side of the vehicle, Edward Cannon had gotten out and was rolling his shoulders.

Charley had no idea he had returned from Europe. But if Dan's father was here, did that mean...?

She grabbed the windowsill, fighting an unexpected rush of alarm. She was not up to a visit from Dan's mother right now.

But when she looked down again, it wasn't Rose who was fighting with the wind for control of the umbrella. Ultimately successful, the woman raised her head and stared directly at Charley's window.

She sank back embarrassed as if she had been caught spying—which, of course, she had.

Who is that?

She peeked out and watched, intrigued, as Arcadi and Ted Cannon, under direction from the stranger, extracted a large steamer trunk, and carried it up the steps to the front door.

What was going on? No one had told her they were having a house guest.

Claire Zammit could wait. She needed to investigate.

"Oh, Charlotte, there you are! Good. Good." Ted's warm smile beamed up at her as she descended the staircase.

She had always liked Dan's father. She hoped the rumours that had been circulating were wrong and that his trip to Europe had yielded the contracts his shipyard desperately needed.

Ted's balding head bobbed excitedly as he looked from her to Bessie and Freddie, who were all standing in the foyer staring at their visitors. "Now we're all here, I can make the proper introductions."

Freddie was smiling at the woman, but Gran looked as dark and stormy as the weather outside.

"Allow me to introduce Lady Evelyn Pierrepont, Countess of—"

"We don't take much stock in aristocratic titles here," Bessie snapped.

"And of course, this is Mrs. Elizabeth Stormont, Mr. Frederick Stormont, and Mrs. Charlotte Hall," Ted stammered out the rest of the introductions as Arcadi deposited a pair of large suitcases beside the steamer trunk. "We met on the ship, returning from England, and were seatmates on the train from Montreal today. I thought it was only sensible that I escort her the rest of the way." He glanced nervously at Bessie. "But I'm sure Rose is anxious for me to be home after all these months, so I'll bid you all *adieu*."

Another time, Charley might have found it humorous just how quickly Ted scampered out of the foyer, down the front steps, and back into Arcadi's cab. Instead, she was still reeling from the realization of who the stranger was.

Evelyn Pierrepont.

Her mother's mother.

Her *other* grandmother.

"Well, is no one going to say anything?" Evelyn Pierrepont said in a pronounced English accent.

"Welcome to Kingston, Grandmama." Freddie took her umbrella and bent to kiss her cheek.

Lady Evelyn Pierrepont had a sharp, angular face. She was thin, almost to the point of emaciation, and Charley wondered if she had always been that way or if the deprivations of the war and its aftermath had taken a toll. She knew things had been harder for the people of Europe. She assumed Evelyn must be close in age to Gran but she looked ten years older with more wrinkles etched into her cheeks and deep creases under a pair of non-descript brown eyes. Her mouth was pierced in what Charley thought of as a permanent look of disapproval.

Then again, she had endured weeks at sea and a four-hour train ride, so she likely wasn't at her best.

Charley stepped off the bottom step. "Welcome, ah..." She didn't know how to address her. "This is an unexpected surprise."

"Is it?" Evelyn's painted-on eyebrows arched as she turned to Freddie.

Charley glanced at Gran whose own mouth was pinched with disapproval.

"It must have slipped my mind," Freddie said, attempting a disarming smile.

He would have been more successful if he didn't smell like a distillery and look like he hadn't slept in days—which he likely hadn't. Charley was surprised her brother was even home—she had seen him so rarely over past the week. He was supposed to start classes yesterday, but she was quite certain his plan to resume his studies had become another victim of his lost sobriety.

"Why don't we go sit in the drawing room," Bessie said. "Rachel? No, leave the luggage as it is. Will you make us some tea, please?"

Evelyn went straight to Charley's favourite chair. But that was fine. Charley sat down on the couch beside Gran, and took her hand, a united front against the intruder—at least that seemed to be how Bessie was interpreting the visit. If lines were going to be drawn, Charley knew whose side she wanted to be on.

"Now, why don't you tell us why you're here, Evelyn?" Despite the challenge in the question, Bessie had put on her best hostess voice.

"I invited her," Freddie said.

"You what?" Charley wished she could emulate Gran's calm demeanour, but Freddie's admission shocked her.

"I wrote to her after we learned the truth about how Mother and Father died. She had a right to know."

A right she gave up when she disowned her own daughter for marrying Charley's father, according to Gran.

Still, Freddie had a point. Evelyn did deserve to know her daughter had been murdered and the culprit revealed. She wished she—or Bessie—had thought to inform her. That it had been Freddie who had done so...well, it didn't seem to be the kind of attention to detail he usually bothered with.

"Quite right," Bessie said. "But I hardly think the information warranted an Atlantic crossing."

"I thought it was high time I got to know my grandchildren," Evelyn said. "They are adults, so I assume you are now willing to let them decide for themselves what kind of relationship they wish to have with their Grandmama."

Grandmama.

Charley couldn't imagine calling Evelyn that—couldn't imagine using any form of familial endearment with this stranger.

Rachel wheeled in a tea wagon and proceeded to pour out four cups of tea after first inquiring if milk or sugar was desired. "Biscuits?" she asked after distributing the cups.

"Leave them on the table, please. We'll serve ourselves," Gran said when no one accepted.

Evelyn took a sip from her cup. "Lovely," she said. "You make an excellent cup of tea, Rachel."

Rachel turned pink and curtsied. "Thank you, Lady Thorton."

Gran's teacup rattled in its saucer. Charley turned sharply towards her. She had noticed it, too.

Lady Thorton.

How did Rachel know Evelyn Pierrepont's aristocratic title?

Bessie recovered first. She put down her teacup and turned a disapproving glare on their guest. "It is customary, in this country at least, for an invitation to be issued before one arrives on a doorstep expecting lodging and hospitality." Her tone was cool.

"I told you, I invited her," Freddie said, petulantly. "It's my house, too. I can invite whomever I wish."

Charley waited for Bessie to correct him, but instead, she said, "Of course you may. I merely would have appreciated the courtesy of being informed in order to prepare properly for the visit." She turned to Evelyn. "How long will we have the pleasure of your company?"

"I've booked return passage for when the ships resume their sailing schedule in the spring." She turned to Freddie. "I've booked it for two."

Gran leapt to her feet, her expression as fierce as any mother fighting to protect her child. She had raised Charley and Freddie after their parents' deaths twenty-five years earlier. It was obvious to Charley that Bessie viewed Evelyn's arrival as a threat to the integrity of her family.

"What are you playing at, Evelyn?" Bessie's tone was challenging—a shot across the bow.

Evelyn raised her chin defiantly. "My husband and son are both dead, and Freddie is the sole heir to the earldom. As I told him when he left England to sail for Canada in '46, it is imperative that he return to the Midlands to claim his birthright. Either he becomes the ninth Earl of Thorton or the title becomes extinct."

An ill wind, indeed.

Things aren't looking good for Charley. What's next?

When the man who replaced Charley on the city beat asks for help, she hopes it will prove to her editor she's a serious reporter. But when a city official turns up dead and a baby is kidnapped, she fears her reporting may be responsible. Now everyone is under suspicion and Charley faces her darkest days since the war when her husband went missing.

Get *Odds on Murder* to see if it's the jackpot or snake eyes for Charley! Keep reading for a sneak peek.

⸺ ⸺

If you enjoyed *A Diagnosis of Murder*, please consider leaving a review on the site of your favourite e-retailer or GoodReads so that others can find out about the Charley Hall historical mystery series.

Is this your first Charley Hall Mystery? Get *A Shot of Murder*, book 1 in the series, and follow Charley and the gang from the beginning.

Want more from Charley and her friends? Head over to my website and sign up for the *Gayle Gazette* to keep up-to-date on new releases, exclusive access to special features and giveaways. Plus, you'll get a free download of a solve-it-yourself *Bessie Stormont Whodunit*. Yup, Gran has some real detective skills, too.

HISTORICAL NOTES

While *A Diagnosis of Murder* is fiction, some incidents and inspirations in the story are rooted in fact.

HEAT WAVE

At the end of August 1948, a heat wave gripped parts of Ontario and the United States. Lasting over a week, temperatures in Kingston rose as high as 91°F (32.8°C), the hottest in three years, and unusual for the lakeside town. Some offices closed early, beaches were crowded, and many flocked to the countryside as people tried to escape the heat.

NURSES' REUNION

On August 4, 5, and 6, 1948, the 1946 graduating class of Hotel Dieu Hospital nurses held a reunion. According to the *Kingston Whig-Standard* (August 11, 1948, p. 9): "On Friday, Miss A. Forestell and Miss V. Shields were joint hostesses at a luncheon and at three o'clock, a tea, sponsored by Sister Hughes, superintendent of nurses, was served by student nurses. Mrs. M. McKinnon, president of the Nurses' Alumnae, poured." There were twelve nurses present. There is no report of any of them falling ill or dying.

SERVICES AT DIEPPE

In August 1948, seventy-five former servicemen, many accompanied by their wives, took part in ceremonies at Dieppe, France, to commemorate the raid on the town by Canadian Forces, August 19, 1942. The activities described in the novel were reported in the newspaper. (*Kingston Whig-Standard*, August 20, 1948, p. 13).

SNEAK PEEK: ODDS ON MURDER

A CHARLEY HALL MYSTERY, BOOK 4

CHARLEY HALL COULD FEEL his breath on her neck. She kept her head down and focused on completing the paragraph she was typing on the portable, red Smith-Corona typewriter she carted back and forth to the office most days. Focus was something she'd become very good at after six years of working in the noisy newsroom of the *Kingston Tribune*.

Why was he bothering her anyway? She was an hour away from deadline. If she ignored him, maybe he'd go away.

He cleared his throat.

Then again, when was the last time he'd approached her desk? He preferred to bellow at her from across the newsroom.

She stopped typing and slowly spun her chair to look up into the bespectacled eyes of John Sherman, the *Trib*'s managing editor. "Can I help you with something?" she said, her sweet voice dripping with sarcasm.

"Can you come to my office?" he said quietly.

"Now? I have to finish this piece on royal baby fashion."

"What's that?"

Charley sighed at the incredulity she saw on his face. This was hardly the type of hard news she wanted to be writing, either, but Princess Elizabeth had just given birth to her first child, a son and future king, and—trivial or not—readers of the women's pages would expect *something* on the subject. "Never mind." She stood. "Let's go."

"Close the door," Sherman said, taking his seat behind his desk. He didn't ask her to sit down. She rarely did in his office. It was a power-play between them. A self-conscious, five-foot-four Sherman had his desk and chair raised on blocks so he could appear to look down at visitors seated across from him. Charley, at five-foot-seven, preferred to remain standing. It was difficult enough being the *Trib*'s only female reporter; she'd take any advantage she could.

Patience didn't come easy to her, but she was learning to hone that particular skill. It came in handy when researching a story. Or investigating a murder. Recently, Charley had found herself embroiled in several murder investigations—the first one implicating her older brother, Freddie, and the second one, her best friend, Dan. Well, Dan used to be her best friend but that was up for debate at the moment. And then there was that trouble at the hospitals.

Charley waited while Sherman fiddled with a pile of papers on his desk, his eyes periodically darting up at her. Finally, he expelled a long breath and asked, "Have you seen Pyne recently?"

The question caught her totally off guard. Lester Pyne. Her nemesis. The bane of her existence. Okay, so that was a little over-dramatic, but the man had taken her job as city reporter, relegating her to the women's pages. "No," she said. And then before she could stop herself, "Why?"

Darn it! The question slipped past her lips automatically.

Sherman's sharp-eyed gaze pinned her. "He hasn't been in the office for a few days."

"I hadn't noticed." Behind her back, her fingers crossed as a superstitious take-back of the lie. Of course, she'd noticed. She noticed everything Lester Pyne did and didn't do. She needed the right opportunity to prove to Sherman that the man wasn't up to the job—*her* job.

"I'd like you to go around and check on him."

"Me?" Her voice squeaked.

"Yeah, you." He pushed the wire-rimmed glasses up onto his head and rubbed his eyes. "If it's something to do with a story he's working on, you might be able to help him."

"And if it's not?"

He shrugged. "It would be better coming from a woman. I mean, if he's dealing with...you know..."

She waited.

"If it's something personal," he snapped. "Maybe he's having trouble adjusting to civilian life. You have experience with that."

Charley sank onto the couch. Yes, she had experience with that. Her brother, Freddie. Two-and-a-half years after VE day and he still couldn't talk about what had happened to him over there, let alone tell her what had happened to her husband. How could she expect a complete stranger to do so? And frankly, she wasn't sure she'd even want him to.

"I don't know where he lives." *Darn!* Surely, she could have come up with something better.

Sherman, of course, pounced on her feeble excuse. "Talk to Miss Fletcher. She can give you his home address, and the story he was working on." He lowered his glasses and opened a file on his desk, dismissing her.

Miss Fletcher.

Grace.

The *Tribune's* archivist was the only person John Sherman showed any real deference to. Probably because he knew the place would collapse without her. With a degree in library science, she'd joined the staff not long after Charley to manage the mountain of information the reporters generated and to catalogue articles from all the *Trib's* published editions. However, she'd quickly proven to be a top-notch researcher, too. Grace could ferret out those seemingly innocuous details that would break a story wide open. And she was the only other woman working for the newspaper.

Charley pushed open the door to the archives—known as the morgue—and called out to her friend.

"Oh good." Grace tucked a wayward strand of her long, blonde hair behind her ear. "I found some old baby photographs of Princess Elizabeth and her sister, Margaret, which I thought you could use with your article. Here, let me show you." She slipped off her stool and walked over to a long counter where she'd arranged a series of images.

Charley scanned them briefly. "Thanks, these are great. But they're not why I'm here."

Grace leaned back against the counter and cocked her head, her pale blue eyes concerned. "Is something wrong? Is it Freddie?"

She shook her head. "No, Freddie seems to be doing better since Laine was moved up to the fourth floor."

Grace looked away and tried to surreptitiously wipe at a tear. Dr. Laine Black, Grace's dear friend and roommate, had been grievously injured a few months earlier and had spent several weeks in a coma, kept alive by a mechanical respirator. She was making slow progress toward recovery, but she'd had a serious head injury, and no one could say whether or not she would ever return to the intelligent, vivacious woman she'd been before. A few weeks previous, she'd been moved from intensive care on the second floor up to the fourth floor, which housed the shell-shocked soldiers who'd returned from the war—many of whom had once been her patients.

"He's been reading to her, you know," Grace said.

That was news to Charley. Thanks to Grace and Laine —and a sailboat christened as the *Lady Pierrepont*—her brother had finally seemed to be overcoming his alcohol addiction until the attack on Laine had sent him back to the bottle. "I had no idea. I did know he had started that new sobriety program that's been in the news."

"Yes. And he's resumed his studies at Queen's University." Grace peered at Charley. "You didn't know?"

"I haven't spoken to him much these past few months." Charley didn't add that Freddie was deliberately avoiding her and Gran—and well he should after the stunt he'd pulled after Labour Day.

"Well, if it's not Freddie and it's not Laine, why are you looking so glum?"

"Lester Pyne."

Grace's eyes widened in surprise and she turned away to stack and straighten the princesses' baby photographs.

"Grace?"

The archivist picked up a pencil and turned back to Charley. "What about him?"

"John Sherman asked me to check on him."

"He asked you? Why?"

"I don't know. Because he hasn't been in for a few days, and I guess Sherman's worried. Now, you're making me think there might be something to it."

Grace hesitated, tapping her pencil against her thigh.

Something was going on. Grace was never this secretive —not with her, and not about Lester Pyne, whom they both agreed shouldn't have stolen Charley's job. "C'mon, Grace, what gives?"

Grace turned to the counter and scribbled onto a notepad. Then she tore off the sheet and handed it to Charley. "This is his home address."

"I was going to telephone him, not pay him a social call," Charley said in a dry tone.

Grace shook her head. "Better to go see him. I wouldn't trust the telephone."

Now Charley was really curious. "Do you know what he was working on?"

Grace nodded and handed her a manila-coloured envelope. Charley opened it and withdrew a single typewritten page. She recognized it immediately.

She scanned the document, but there was no more information now than there had been when Grace had shown it to her several months ago. "Colin Banks?"

"Lester came to me a month ago and asked me to see what I could find out about him. I gave him what I had dug up for you. He thinks it's odd, too, that there is nothing about him before he arrived in Kingston two years ago."

Charley's reporter instincts wondered if she'd let a scoop get away—lost an opportunity to get her old job back. But Grace hadn't given her the information for a story. It had been personal. And it wasn't Colin Banks she'd been interested in, anyway; it was his sister, Meredith—the woman whose engagement to her childhood friend, Alderman Dan Cannon, had both stunned and devastated her. They'd barely spoken since the announcement.

"Has he found anything?" Charley asked.

Grace shrugged. "All I know is that it's Wednesday and no one has heard from him since he left here Friday night."

Now it was making sense. "You alerted Sherman."

Grace nodded. "He doesn't keep close tabs on his reporters' comings and goings, as you well know. All he cares about is getting a scoop. I'm sorry, Charley, I didn't think you'd be the one he'd ask to check up on Lester. But I'm worried. It's not like Lester to be out of touch for so long. He's still a fairly new reporter. What if he's gotten in over his head...or something worse has happened to him?"

Want to read more? Get *Odds on Murder*, book 4 in the Charley Hall Mystery series today!

ACKNOWLEDGEMENTS

Writing is a solitary pursuit but publishing a book is not. I am forever grateful to two talented author/editors who are instrumental in bringing my stories to you.

Joanna D'Angelo, my friend and editor, who suggested I write a mystery series and brainstormed ideas with me during a long drive to Toronto and back—and then hounded me until I actually wrote it.

Carolyn Heald, a historian, archivist and talented writer in her own right, she is also—and truly fortunate for me—an excellent copy editor who is very familiar with the city of Kingston as well as proper grammar.

In addition, over the past year I have been supported by the great team at Best Page Forward, who have taught me so much about the self-publishing world.

Finally, I want to express my sincere appreciation to the members of the Ottawa Romance Writers, the Women's Fiction Writers Association, Crime Writers of Canada, and Sisters in Crime, who provide unconditional support and a safe space to ask questions in this strange world of fiction writing.

ABOUT BRENDA GAYLE

I've been a writer all my life but returned to my love of fiction after more than 20 years in the world of corporate communications—although some might argue there is plenty of opportunity for fiction-writing there, too. I have a Master's degree in journalism and an undergraduate degree in psychology. A fan of many genres, I find it hard to stay within the publishing industry's prescribed boxes. Whether it's historical mystery, romantic suspense, or women's fiction, my greatest joy is creating deeply emotional books with memorable characters and compelling stories.

Connect with me on my website at BrendaGayle.com & sign up for *The Gayle Gazette,* my newsletter, to keep up-to-date on new releases, exclusive access to special features, giveaways, and all sorts of shenanigans. And don't forget, as a subscriber, you'll get a free download of a *Bessie Stormont Whodunit.*

Until next time...

ALSO BY BRENDA GAYLE

CHARLEY HALL MYSTERY SERIES

A Shot of Murder

Rigged for Murder

A Diagnosis of Murder

Odds on Murder

Murder in Abstract

Schooled in Murder